The Slow Road to Hell

by Grant Atherton

with grateful thanks to

JAKOB PAULUSSEN

for all his valuable help and advice

Cover art by
SelfPubBookCovers.com/BeeJavier

Grant Atherton's Website
GrantAtherton.co.uk

WARNING

This book contains sexually explicit scenes and adult language and may be considered offencive to some readers.

The Slow Road to Hell, Copyright (c) May, 2017 by Grant Atherton

All rights reserved. No part of this book may be reproduced, scanned or distributed in any printed or electronic form without prior written permission for the author. Please do not participate in or encourage piracy of copyrighted materials in violation of the author's rights. Purchase only authorised editions.

This book is a work of fiction. While reference might be made to actual historical events or existing locations, the names, characters, places and incidents are either the product of the author's imagination or are used fictitiously, and any resemblance to actual persons, living or dead, business establishments, events or locales is entirely coincidental.

CHAPTER ONE

"She's lying. You see that?" I jabbed a finger at the image on the monitor screen. "You see how she reacted?"

Inspector Denby squinted at the screen and scratched his chin. "You're going to have to talk me through that, Mikey. All I see is a young woman under a lot of stress."

We were sitting around a desk in Denby's office in London's City Road Police Station. There were four of us; me, Denby, and two of his officers. They had been working this case for over two weeks and getting nowhere. That's when I'd been called in at the behest of Denby's Chief and much to the chagrin of Denby. I was the last resort. The witch doctor. I read people. And right then I was reading Lydia Carson, the wife - correction, widow - of Ray Carson, recently deceased, found lying in a pool of blood on his kitchen floor.

Lydia Carson was the sole suspect. Exhaustive enquiries had disclosed no other viable suspects, and no possible motive. And that left just Lydia. The nearest and dearest. Always the top of any murder enquiry suspect list.

Trouble was, there was nothing to suggest it was her either. By all accounts the Carsons were rarely seen out of each other's company in public and had never been known to quarrel or behave in any way that suggested anything other than a close loving relationship.

But every move she made, every reaction, told me she was hiding something.

"You have to know what to look for," I said. "Sure, she's stressed. You've been grilling her for nearly three hours. Who wouldn't be stressed? But you have to look past that. You have to look for those idiosyncrasies, those patterns of behaviour that tell us what's really going on."

"I don't doubt you, Mikey. I just don't see what you see."

Men like Denby were always slow to embrace new methods, methods like mine, always going to kick back against anything they didn't understand.

"I'll show you." I leaned toward the microphone on the desk and said, "Dave, it's Mikey. I'm coming in."

On the screen, Sgt David Brady, the interviewing officer, nodded imperceptibly, continuing to speak to the woman seated on the other side of his desk.

I'd worked with Brady before when he was over at the Bethnal Green Station and we'd gotten to know each other well. He was one of the more forward-thinking officers, already a supporter of my techniques, and I knew he wouldn't mind my breaking into his interview.

A few moments later, I opened the door of the interview room and stepped inside.

Lydia Carson was in her early thirties, short dark hair with a fringe she constantly brushed from her face - a sign of her nervousness - and was dressed in a plain grey but well-cut trouser suit.

I smiled at her. "Hello, Lydia. I'm Michael MacGregor and I'd like to ask you some questions if that's okay."

She blinked up at me and then turned to face Dave Brady, her eyebrows knitted.

He didn't respond.

Turning back to me, she said, "I don't understand. I've just been through it all again. You keep asking me the same questions over and over and I don't know what else I can tell you."

I drew back a chair and sat down, facing Lydia from the other side of the desk. "I'm not here to interview you, Lydia. I'm not a policeman. I leave the interviewing to people like Sgt Brady here."

I gave a casual nod in his direction. Brady folded his arms and leaned back in his chair.

"I'm a Forensic Psychologist," I continued. "And I'm here to ask for your help."

Lydia's hand went to her throat. "A Psychologist? Why would I need to speak to a Psychologist?"

"Let me explain." I spread my hands before me on the desk. "It's my job to build up a profile of the person who did this. Try to get some idea of what he's like. It helps us to focus in on the kind of person we're looking for."

She swallowed hard and dropped her hand. "But I have no idea ... I don't know ..."

I interrupted. "We start with what we do know, the information we already have. And what we have are the details of the crime scene."

"I don't understand."

"Well, for instance, we can assume with a safe degree of certainty that Ray either knew his killer, or it was someone he wouldn't feel threatened by. There was no forced entry so it would appear he was invited in. And from what we know of Ray, he was no weakling was he? He would have been able to handle himself if there had been some sort of immediate threat."

Lydia lowered her gaze and stared down at the table. "Yes, I suppose so."

"And if there had been a confrontation, it's more likely to have happened near the point of entry, in the hallway, and there would have been signs of disturbance. But Ray was attacked in the kitchen at the back of the house. So it's reasonable to presume that the killer was allowed access. Again, this suggests there was no immediate conflict, that it was someone Ray would have no cause to feel threatened by. Okay so far?"

Lydia looked up again.

I said, "It's strange that a visitor would have been invited into the kitchen anyway. The domestic centre of the house. It would have been more usual to have been shown into the living room."

I paused.

She blinked and remained silent.

"But no matter," I said. "We'll let that go for the moment. What concerns me more is the murder weapon, the knife."

"They never found it," Lydia volunteered.

"That's right. And that's where I'm going to need your help. You see, if the killer came into the house with a knife, it's a fairly safe bet he was expecting trouble, that maybe he intended to use the knife, to protect himself from a threat or to threaten Ray, or he may have intended from the start to harm Ray. If, on the other hand, the knife was already there, in the kitchen, that's a different matter. Do you see what I'm saying? It would show that this wasn't premeditated. That it may well have been a spur of the moment thing. It's important because it gives us some indication of the killer's original intention, his possible state of mind when he arrived at the house. So, if you could be absolutely certain about whether or not any knives are missing, it would be a great help."

Lydia brushed the hair from her forehead. "I understand what you're asking but I don't think I can help. As far as I know, none of the kitchen knives are missing. But I can't be sure."

"Okay. But you appreciate what I'm getting at here? How all these different aspects of the crime can help us build a picture of the killer?"

"I understand. I just wish I could be more help."

"And then there's Ray himself. The sort of man he was. That could have an effect on the killer's reaction to him. The way he would act in any given situation. Would he stay calm? Get agitated? Lose his temper? Maybe even become violent? His actions could affect the killer's response."

"I see what you mean but I have no idea how he would have reacted."

Again, Lydia's hand went to her throat. She stroked her neck and then averted her gaze and looked down at the table.

I waited.

She raised her eyes again.

"Let me tell you a bit more about the kind of work I do. Do you understand the concept of body language?"

Lydia furrowed her brows. "I've heard of it, yes. But I don't know much about it."

"Well, when we communicate with others, less than fifty percent of what we pass on is verbal. Most of the messages we communicate to others are non-verbal. Through our bodies. And we all have our own little quirks that give away what we're thinking and feeling. Our own 'tells'. So, for instance, if you say something I don't agree with, I may well fold my arms in front of my chest, a sort of defensive barrier. It's something I would do to express my disagreement. But it's something I would do subconsciously, without realising it. You understand?"

"I think so."

"And because we do these things subconsciously, we don't have any control over them. So even if we tell a lie, our bodies still tell the truth." I leaned closer to emphasise my next point. "And this is the most interesting thing, Lydia. After years of studying other people's behaviour, you know what I've discovered?"

She shook her head.

"Everybody lies. Everybody. There's no such thing as a completely honest person." I leaned back in my chair. "Of course, we all lie for different reasons. So for instance, if we were interviewing someone we suspected of committing a crime, he may well lie to avoid being caught."

"I suppose that's obvious."

"Yes, but then there are the others. Innocent people lie too. Maybe out of fear, or shame or embarrassment. Are you still with me?"

"I think so."

"And I was wondering, Lydia, if that's why you've been lying. If maybe there's something you're frightened to admit or something you're embarrassed about."

A gasp escaped her lips. "I don't know what you mean." Her voice trembled. "I've told you everything I can."

I dismissed her claim with a wave of the hand. "I'll tell you how I know, shall I? You see, I've studied your previous taped interviews and I've been able to build up a picture of your personal 'tells', the way your body reacts. Shall I tell you what they are?"

She didn't respond. Just stared at me, wide eyed.

"There's this thing you do with your feet. When you tell a lie, you wrap them around the legs of the chair. It's something we call 'anchoring'. It's an innate subconscious attempt to cover something up, to hide it. And after you've done that, you immediately raise your hand and stroke your neck. That's something we call a 'pacifying' action. A soothing action. An attempt to calm yourself after doing something dishonest, such as telling a lie."

Once again, Lydia raised a hand to her throat.

I pointed to the hand. "See, you just did it. You didn't even think about it. It was a reflex action. That's how I know you've been lying. And this is the interesting part. These signs that give you away, your personal tells, mostly seem to be when you're talking about Ray, about the sort of person he was. And that's how I know Ray wasn't the kind, peaceable guy you like to claim he was. So why don't you tell us what he was really like, Lydia. What it is you're too afraid to tell?"

She stared at me, mouth half open. And then she burst into tears, collapsed onto the table, and buried her face in her hands, crying openly. Her shoulders shook with each gasping sob.

I leaned toward her and lowered my voice. "Let me tell you what I think happened, Lydia. I think you reached breaking point. I think you grew tired of pretending, of hoping that everything would be all right. I think you'd had enough."

She raised her head, still sobbing, and wiped a hand across her eyes. "I couldn't take any more. I just couldn't. I'd only been gone half an hour. Only to the shops. But he was screaming at me. Calling me names. Wanting to know where I'd been. Calling me a liar. And then he came at me, raised his fists. And I just couldn't go through it again. Not again. And the knife was on the work top beside me. I didn't even stop to think. I just picked it up and lashed out. I just wanted to stop him. That's all. And the next moment, he was on the floor. And there was so much blood."

"It's all right, Lydia," I said, trying to calm her. "No one is making any judgements here. Just tell Sgt Brady what happened and then we can start to put things right. Start at the beginning and the sergeant here will take it all down. Just take your time." I pushed back the chair. "Sgt Brady will take good care of you."

I made my excuses, signalled farewell to Dave, and left Lydia to make her statement, sobbing as she did so.

A little while later, I was on my way out of the station, having said my goodbyes to Denby and his men.

There are times this work depresses me. This kind of case most of all. There were too many women like Lydia, living fearful secret lives. And now she would have to live through the nightmare ahead.

As I made it out of the door, I checked my mobile. Four missed calls. All from Karen. Karen was one of my oldest friends and we often chatted on the 'phone. But four missed calls? Something had to be wrong, and I had a feeling I was about to get even more depressed.

I called her back.

She sounded distressed. "Mikey it's your father. I'm worried."

CHAPTER TWO

By the time the police arrived, I was nursing a painfully swollen shoulder. Breaking down doors had never been high on my list of skills and now I knew it never would be. Something I wish I'd known before I tried it.

It's not like in the movies where the muscle-bound hero shoulders one a couple of times and sends it flying off its hinges. Not a chance. Not that I was without a few muscles myself but in the event, all I managed to do was badly bruise my shoulder and my ego, and make enough noise to send the neighbours scurrying for the phone to call the police.

Which is why I was now standing outside the door of my father's vicarage in the company of Sgt Richard Lowe of Elders Edge constabulary waiting for the local locksmith to let us in.

"You sure he's inside?" asked Lowe. He blew into his cupped hands and then rubbed them together, clearly not too happy about standing around in the bitter cold of the open courtyard.

"Where else would he be? I've tried everywhere I can think of." I looked at him askance. What did he think I was doing here? Did he think I threw myself at doors for fun?

"Family?"

"I'm all he has left."

"And he couldn't be staying with friends?"

Friends? My father? That was a joke. He'd alienated all the friends he'd had a long time ago. "Not that I know of." This guy was testing my patience. "Look Sergeant, I wasn't prepared to wait around on the off chance he turned up. He's not been in the best of health and I was worried."

"Wouldn't he have called you if he'd been ill?"

"No."

"Oh?"

"I've already explained. I no longer live locally."

"You don't stay in touch?"

"We haven't spoken for several months. We're not close."

"Oh?"

That was one 'oh' too many, and it irritated me. Sgt Lowe had shown way too much interest in my personal affairs since he'd arrived. "It's a long story," I said, and turned away, determined to avoid any further interrogation.

I fixed my attention on Mr Dawson, the locksmith, as he loaded his drill and stepped into the shelter of the arched porch. I was eager for him to finish so I could get out of the chill February air. It was that dull dispiriting time of year when the festive season was a distant memory and it seemed like spring would never come. The constant drizzle of rain had stopped but a cold wind persisted, blowing in from over the coast road to the east. All sensation of warmth had long since drained from my limbs. I wrapped my arms around my chest and stamped my feet on the stone flags.

"I'll soon be done," said Dawson, clearly interpreting my actions as a sign of impatience. Not that he was far wrong.

"So what brings you down here now?" Lowe asked.

"I got a call from a friend. She was worried. She's not seen my father around for a few days and wondered if I knew where he was. I didn't. Nor did anyone else. The rest you know. I drove down to check up on him."

"This friend? Someone who knows him well? She'd know if something was amiss?"

I turned my full attention back to Lowe and tried to read his expression. What was it with this guy? Was he compiling a dossier on me or was this his idea of small talk? The craggy face was expressionless.

Over the sound of Dawson's drilling, I said, "She knows him well enough to be concerned when he's not been seen around for a few days. Karen Dyer. She runs the Fairview guest house over on the Esplanade. I'm sure she'll be only too happy to confirm what I've told you."

"Karen? I know Karen. She's a friend of yours?" He sounded surprised. Like it was something he should have known about.

"I've known Karen all my life. We grew up together."

"You're quite close then?"

"Yes." What else was I hearing here? Why this sudden interest in my relationship with Karen? My turn to be nosey. "You know Karen well?"

He flushed. "I ... er ... yes, I guess."

"Oh?" Time to get my own back.

"We've been seeing each other."

"Oh?" Interesting. So our nosey Sergeant fancied his chances.

I took a closer look at our boy in blue. Not a bad looking guy. Medium height and a bit on the thin side. But Karen could have done worse. Under the regulation helmet was a sharp hawkish face. Chiselled features and carbon-black eyes under dark bushy brows.

Whatever was going on between them, I hoped she'd made a better choice this time.

He said, "We get on well together."

"Really?" I was enjoying this.

Fortunately for Lowe, he was saved from any further embarrassment by the sound of the door lock dropping onto the stone floor of the porch. Dawson turned off his drill and stepped back into view, a look of triumph on his face. "All done," he said.

Lowe was ahead of me. He approached the door and pushed it open. The church tower, stark and unprepossessing, that ever watchful guardian over my childhood virtues, looked down on us from over the top of the vicarage roof as I closed in behind him. How I hated it.

On the threshold, we were greeted by a malodorous smell from inside the house which brought us both to a halt. It wasn't a smell I was familiar with but I had no doubt about its cause. Lowe probably recognised it too. I suppose in his line of work, he may have been around a dead body or two in his time. It was the pungent odour of rotting flesh with a hint of sickening sweetness.

It was all too obvious what was waiting for us inside. My stomach churned, and I gripped the door jamb to steady myself. I clasped a hand over my mouth and pinched my nose but nothing could block out that noisome stench.

A gust of wind blew in from the coast, carrying with it the

faint far off sound of the sea, of waves breaking against the distant shore. We stood together for a few moments, not speaking.

Lowe was the first to move. He stepped over the threshold and I followed him through the gloomy hallway to the living room where the smell was strongest. We entered the room, and I tried to push past him but he held me back with an outstretched arm.

"Best not touch anything," he said.

As if I would.

My father was seated in his old battered armchair by the fireside. The ashes of a recent fire covered the hearth grate. He was dressed casually, faded brown corduroy trousers and a baggy brown cardigan. As ever, he wore his clerical collar, the symbol of his presumed authority to sit in judgement over the rest of us. Something I remembered all too well.

He looked, for all the world, as if he had settled down for a rest at the end of the day, his shock of white hair resting against the back of the chair, his lined face in repose.

The room was cold, and I shivered.

I wasn't sure what I'd expected to find. But not this. My father had been in poor health - a couple of heart attacks had a way of knocking the wind out of your sails - and I'd presumed he was laid up in bed. Maybe in need of help. But not this. I hoped it had been quick. That he hadn't suffered.

He stared up at me, dead eyes full of blame, and an overpowering sense of guilt and loss welled up inside me.

I turned away, heart racing, and made my way outside, took in a few deep breaths of cold fresh air and gazed out into the distance, not seeing anything.

He hadn't been the best of fathers. God knows we'd had little cause to like each other over the past few years. But maybe I hadn't been the best of sons. There was a time when perhaps I could have tried harder, found a way to work out our differences and get along.

But then he'd found out about Nathan. And after that, I'm not sure anything could be the same again. Maybe if I'd tried. Maybe if we'd both tried. And now I'd never know.

Over to my right, a net curtain twitched in the window of the only other house in the courtyard. It was, as previously pointed out by Sgt Lowe, the home of my father's current Curate, Giles Trivett, the concerned citizen who had called the police. Trivett lived there with his wife, Frances, but I couldn't tell which of them was at the window.

Given the proximity of people who took such an obvious interest in the comings and goings at their neighbour's house, how had my father been left undiscovered for so long? Surely, his non-appearance would have prompted any reasonable person to check in on him before now. Especially his own Curate, living right next door.

A hand on my shoulder interrupted my thoughts. It was Lowe. "Looks like a heart attack."

I nodded, unable to speak. Dawson made clucking sounds and looked embarrassed.

Lowe said, "I'll take care of this. Dawson can fit a new lock and I'll leave the keys with Trivett." He nodded in the direction of the Curate's house. "Just let me know where I can get in touch with you to make arrangements about the ... about your father's remains."

I pulled myself together. "I'll go down to the Fairview. Karen should have a spare room at this time of year. You have the number?"

"I have it. Go get yourself settled and we'll touch base later."

CHAPTER THREE

I dropped my bags by the reception desk in the lobby.

The place hadn't changed much.

The Fairview was one of those old-fashioned privately run seaside guest houses you didn't see much of any more. It could have used a lick of paint here and there but it was that air of faded gentility that gave the place its charm.

A flame-haired woman appeared from a doorway behind the desk and greeted me with an enthusiastic welcome and open arms.

"Mikey, it's so good to see you."

Karen Dyer was a vibrant attractive woman; sun-kissed and freckled with high cheekbones, and aqua-green eyes in an oval animated face framed by a cascade of untamed hair tumbling down over her shoulders.

I reached out and hugged her. At a time like this, it was good to have a friend like Karen around.

I couldn't remember a time when I hadn't known her. Right from the earliest days of our childhood, she had been one of my closest friends. There had been the three of us; Karen, Nathan and me. We'd played together, laughed together, fought together. We had been inseparable. Those happy carefree days before the world closed in on us and everything changed.

I'd been the first to leave, fleeing to London after that final devastating showdown with my father. I'd resumed my friendship with Karen when she'd married and moved to London some time later. But she'd had a rough ride over the past few years. Life with an alcoholic husband had worn her down until she had finally escaped from the ruins of her marriage and returned to Elders Edge to help her grandmother run the Fairview.

When her grandmother died, she'd inherited the business and kept it going. The life suited her and she looked a damn sight better for it. We had seen each other only occasionally during the past few years whenever she'd travelled down to London. But we'd always kept up a long-distance relationship.

She pulled away, holding me at arm's length. The warmth faded from her eyes. "It's bad news, isn't it? Your father?"

I didn't need to say anything. Karen knew me well enough to read my moods, and my expression would have confirmed what she must have already guessed.

"Heart attack," I said.

"Is he ...?"

"'Fraid so."

"Oh, Mikey, I'm so sorry." She squeezed my arm.

Outside, the wind soughed through the trees and rattled the doors and windows as it circled the house.

"Come on," she said. "We may as well make ourselves comfortable. Let's sit and talk."

She steered me over to a recessed alcove on the other side of the lobby.

A couple of sagging armchairs dressed with carefully ironed antimacassars flanked a panelled fireplace. We settled ourselves into them. A brass companion set stood in the hearth, reflecting the log fire that crackled and blazed in the grate. The warmth of the fire was a welcome relief from the winter chill outside.

"Tell me what I can do," she said.

"Right now I need a room for a few nights. I guess there'll be a lot to sort out so I need to stay around for a while."

"You've got it. I'm officially closed for the winter so we'll have the place to ourselves."

"Good. I'm not sure I'm up to facing people right now."

"How are you taking it?"

"Not sure. Mixed. You know how it was with us. It's not like we'd ever been close. And after ... you know ... what happened ..." I lapsed into silence.

A log cracked and settled in the grate, sending a shower of sparks flying into the air.

I said, "I can't understand why I feel so guilty. As if I'm to blame."

"I suppose while your father was still alive, there was always the possibility of a reconciliation, a chance to put things right between you. And now that chance has gone. It's bound to have an effect, make you feel you've failed somehow."

"I guess so."

"So what happens now?"

"Not too sure. Your Sergeant Lowe said he'd get in touch."

"My Sergeant Lowe?"

I gave her an old-fashioned look.

"What's he been saying?"

Grateful for a change of subject, I said, "He didn't have to say anything. He gave himself away by colouring up every time your name was mentioned. A bit like you're doing now."

Karen pulled a face.

I leaned back in my chair and folded my arms. The worn springs squeaked under my weight. "Well, I'm waiting. Tell me all about it."

"There's nothing to tell. Not really."

"Not really?"

"It's early days yet."

Neither of us had had much luck with relationships so I understood her caution. "I hope it works out. You deserve a break. And he seems like a nice enough bloke."

"We'll see." She forestalled any more questions and said, "And what about you?"

"What about me?"

"I heard about you and Donna. Is it true?"

I grimaced. "She's filing for divorce. My fault."

"No chance of a reconciliation?"

I snorted. "You've got to be joking."

"What happened?"

"The usual. I strayed."

"Oh, Mikey." She glared at me, emphasising her disapproval. "I won't insult you by asking if it was another woman. We both know what a crock that is. So, are you still seeing him?"

I stiffened and sat upright. Karen could still shock me with her directness. I opened my mouth to protest, but the words stuck in my throat and I stammered.

"Don't look so surprised, Mikey. And don't bother to deny it. I've known you a long time and I know you better than you think."

My face burned. She'd always been able to read me like a book. And not always to my advantage.

"Well?" she said.

I sank back into the chair. "It was just one of those things. It wasn't going anywhere."

She clucked. A disparaging sound.

I said, "Shit happens. What can I tell you?"

"Sometimes we make it happen."

"I have a habit of doing that."

"So what will you do now?"

"God knows."

"You're thirty years old, Mikey, and this is your second failed marriage. Doesn't that tell you something?"

"It tells me I'm not very good at relationships. So maybe I should stop trying."

"Well you know what I think."

"I should do. You've told me often enough. But please let's not go there again."

Another well-worn commentary on my dysfunctional life was one thing, but I saw where she was going with this and I needed to head her off. It was the one subject I couldn't discuss. And I wished she could understand why. How painful it would be. I tried to steer her away, but she was having none of it.

"You never ask about him," she said.

"No." I hoped the brusqueness of my response would be enough to deter her from pursuing that particular subject. But no such luck.

"He asks about you," she said.

Her words surprised me. "You stay in touch?"

"Of course we do. You were the one who deserted him."

I turned away and stared down at the fire, watching the dancing flames. On the mantelpiece, a Westminster clock chimed the hour.

I wished she would try to understand why I was so reluctant to go over this again, why it all seemed so pointless. "I don't know what else I could have done."

"Sometimes, Mikey, we have to find the courage to go our own way, no matter what the consequences."

I had nothing to say.

She persisted. "I would have thought, given your background, you'd have more insight into your own nature."

I looked up again. "Maybe I don't want to know."

I was drained. And I didn't want to get into a debate about my many failings.

"Sorry, Karen," I said, "but I'm whacked. Would you mind if we called it a day?"

She rose from her chair, frowning. "Of course not. Come on. I'll fetch you a set of keys while you sign the register and then we'll go find you a room."

CHAPTER FOUR

The face that stared back at me from the bathroom mirror the following morning was pale and drawn; blue eyes rimmed with red and dark-blond hair matted and damp with sweat. I'd seen better looking scarecrows. Groaning inwardly, I stumbled into the shower.

It had been a restless night. Sleep, late coming, had been disturbed by strange unsettling dreams. Elders Edge had worked its baleful magic on my mind, stirring up old memories and painful reminders of a past I would rather forget.

I showered, shaved and dressed, and slipped into a pair of faded Levi's, a cool-blue flannel sweatshirt and a matching blue Arran sweater.

Downstairs, feeling slightly more human, I helped myself to a bowl of Weetabix from Karen's kitchen, knocked back a mug of strong black Gold Blend, and, while the rest of the world was still sleeping, left the Fairview and took the Elan for a drive along the seafront.

Later, I would pick up the vicarage keys from Trivett and then go to the police station to check in with Sgt Lowe. But right then I wasn't ready to deal with the world. I needed some time alone to gather my thoughts and clear my mind.

I slipped the Elan into fourth and sped on out of town along the coast road as dawn's early light streaked the horizon. At the turning to the cliff road, I changed down into first, and took the steep climb to the top.

Night was giving way to day as I walked across the road to the cliff edge.

This was my thinking place. It's where I always came as a young man when I was troubled or needed to work through my problems.

Over to my right, far across the water, the sun was rising to meet the day, staining the sea with a spreading orange glow as it climbed the sky. The morning was clear; the rain that had been forecast was holding off. And although the wind was as strong as ever, it was fresh against my face, clean and invigorating.

Elders Edge spread out below me. All over town, lights went out one by one as darkness retreated and old familiar places emerged into the grey light of day.

From up here, the town had always seemed so small and, by comparison, my problems had always seemed smaller too, so far away.

In its heyday, Elders Edge had been a flourishing Victorian resort, competing favourably with popular spa towns, bringing in holiday-makers from London and other big cities, attracted by the fresh sea air and sandy beaches. It had even boasted a thriving seaport. But all that was in the past. And whilst the town still survived as a holiday destination, its larger grander hotels had closed, the seaport had gone, and visitors came in smaller numbers.

Now that holiday-makers preferred to travel abroad to sunnier climes, seaside resorts like Elders Edge had fallen into decline, and were run-down dilapidated remnants of their former impressive selves.

And how I had always longed to get away from the narrow claustrophobic confines of this worn-out town, the source of all my childhood ills, eager to leave it behind forever. But when that time finally came, it had been a painful and traumatic experience.

In small towns like this, hotbeds of gossip, it was never long before private affairs become the subject of public speculation and so rumours of my relationship with Nathan had reached my father's ears.

I could still hear his words ringing in my head. *You filthy sodomite. You're no son of mine. I hope you rot in hell.* And my mother standing behind him. Face pale. Tears running down her cheeks.

I hadn't denied my feelings. I'd tried to stand up to him. But all those years of conditioning weighed heavy and under that onslaught of invective, the thin tenuous thread of belief I'd clung to had snapped and I'd caved in, accepted his judgement, and promised to change my ways, to strive to be a good and decent son.

It hadn't been easy being raised in a home where hell and damnation were everyday realities where the punishment for breaking the laws of my father's God were harsh and eternal. The growing awareness of my sexuality went hand in hand with feelings of guilt. Was it some sort of punishment? Was I evil? Maybe, in time, I would have been able to come to terms with who and what I was, shake off the yoke of that oppressive doctrine that had been forced on me for as long as I could remember. But it wasn't to be.

We make decisions every day of our lives; big and small, good and bad. And many of them of no lasting significance. But the decision I'd made that day was one I'd learned to regret for many years.

I couldn't have stayed there. Not then. Not under the watchful eye of a father who now despised me no matter how hard I tried to please him. And so I ran away. Packing what few possessions I had, I left without a word to anyone, hurt ashamed and confused. In retrospect, it had been an ill-conceived ill-considered decision. Unhappy and distressed, eager to get away from a home life dominated by a tyrant of a father, and without thinking through the consequences of that decision, I had also left behind the one person who meant more to me than any other. Nathan Quarryman, my friend, confidante and lover.

But there was no going back. Some mistakes cannot be undone. And as time passed, I learned to live with the consequences of that rash decision, making a new life for myself without the man I had loved for nearly half my life. And I tried to forget him.

The town had changed surprisingly little over the years. The Tasty Bites burger bar still propped up the end of the block on Tideswell Road. A favourite eatery of mine until the proprietor, old man Roscoe, caught me emptying the salt cellars into the sugar bowls. Revenge for his refusing to accept he'd shortchanged me. Not that I'd needed a reason. It wouldn't have been the first time I'd pulled some stunt for sheer devilment. Like the time, I'd dropped red dye into the local swimming baths during the school gala. One of many escapades that had provoked my father's wrath. But maybe that was the point. Kickback, I guess, against the pressures of being the vicar's son. And, dear God, there had been some pressures.

Further to the north, the square stone clock tower, nestled within a gated enclosure of cultivated greenery, stood watch over the small paved square where Nathan, Karen and I would often meet up before heading off to a local pub or to take in a film at the Essaldo. The cinema had gone now. A penny arcade stood in its place but the large red Essaldo sign still hung over the entrance on the white stucco facade.

And it was there, in the dark, that my friendship with Nathan had changed into something more. I still remembered that moment. So clearly. We were watching a late night horror film. The three of us. Something with vampires. I sat on one side of Nathan and Karen on the other. As we settled into our seats, Nathan squeezed my leg. As he often did. A friendly gesture. But this time his hand had lingered there, resting on my thigh, and a moment later, I sought his hand and held it. Such a simple gesture. But it changed everything. And it had seemed so right. I don't remember much about that film. Just lots of teeth and blood. But I remembered the way my heart beat against my chest and the way my breath caught in my throat.

I remembered too the times he would join me here. Always knowing where to find me when I needed him. When I was having a hard time with my parents or following some trouble I'd gotten into.

I'd almost forgotten how much I had relied on him. How supportive he'd always been when I needed a friend. The strong arm around my shoulder. The deep reassuring voice.

A tightness gripped my throat and a dull empty ache spread through me. Maybe this hadn't been such a good idea after all. I turned away and made my way back to the car.

CHAPTER FIVE

Storm clouds were already blowing in from over the mainland as I turned into Vicarage Lane. The sky was ashen grey. By the time I reached the vicarage, the first of the rain was falling. I parked up close to the courtyard gate and hurried over to Trivett's house, sidestepping puddles of rainwater and clutching my coat collar against the wind.

The vicarage faced the gate, with Trivett's house to the left, standing at right angles to it. As I neared the two buildings, a uniformed police officer stepped from the shelter of the vicarage porch and took up a position by the entrance.

I stopped and stared at him. The vicarage should have been closed up and secured once my father's body had been removed. So why this? Why would one of Elders Edge's finest be playing guard duty?

I headed towards him.

The uniform spotted me and stood to attention, hands behind his back, his chest puffed out in a display of authority.

He must have thought I was on my way to the vicarage and, when I reached him, he moved to block my approach, and adopted what I presumed was his 'official' pose once more.

"I'm sorry, Sir," he said, "but these premises are off limits at the moment."

"What's the problem here?" I asked.

"No problem, Sir. May I ask you what business it is of yours?"

I explained what business it was of mine. He offered his condolences for my loss but still refused me entry.

I upped my tone a notch and said, "Your Sgt Lowe assured me that I would have access to my father's home this morning. So I'll ask you once again. What's the problem?"

I tried to keep the irritation out of my voice. It was never a good idea to upset the local constabulary.

He drew himself up and said, "With respect, Sir, I wouldn't know anything about that. I was sent here - by Sgt Lowe himself,

I might add - to secure the premises and make sure no one was let in until the Forensics Team had finished their work."

"Forensics?" My heart skipped a beat. "Am I missing something here? My father had a heart attack. Why would you need Forensics?"

"I can't tell you any more, Sir. All I know for sure is that a team is on its way, and I'm here to secure the premises until they arrive. If you need to know anything else, I suggest you get in touch with the station."

"You can be damn sure I will."

All thoughts of hiding my irritation were gone. The dubious pleasure of standing around in the drizzling rain, locking horns with Mr Plod, was fast losing its appeal.

Lowe had meant to leave the vicarage keys with Trivett. Whether or not he had, he may well have appraised Trivett of the current situation.

I took my leave of our boy in blue and made my way over there.

The door opened as I approached. Trivett must have been watching for my arrival. A thin rake of a man stepped out. He wore a pair of cavalry twill trousers, a baggy white woollen pullover that hung off his bony frame like a sail, and a clerical collar. He blinked at me from behind a pair of thick-lensed spectacles which magnified his eyes and gave him the appearance of a startled rabbit.

He greeted me and asked me in. "Sgt Lowe told me to expect you," he explained.

After shaking out my wet coat onto the tiled porch floor, he arranged it on a hook behind the door, and ushered me into the sitting room, fussing around me and keeping up a constant flow of chatter about the bad weather. He was the kind of man who ran on nervous energy. Just watching him was exhausting.

The living room was small and cluttered, with a black leather three-piece suite huddled around a hissing gas fire. Trivett invited me to take a seat on the couch before settling himself into the nearest chair.

The clatter of crockery from nearby suggested that Trivett's wife was taking care of domestic chores in the kitchen.

I hadn't intended to stay but as it was our first acquaintance, it seemed churlish not to. Reluctantly, I sat.

A corner display cabinet to one side of the hearth contained a collection of Dresden figurines and on a sideboard against the adjacent wall, a photograph of a smiling Trivett and an attractive dark-haired woman stared out from a silver frame. His wife? I guessed it must be. Not at all the retiring mousy type I would have expected to partner someone like Trivett. No accounting for taste. But then what would I know. When it came to relationships, on a scale of zero to useless I made it to the top.

With a look of benevolent concern on his face, Trivett proffered his condolences and said, "If I'd known you were Owen's son, I wouldn't have been so hasty in calling the police." His tone was apologetic. "Indeed, your father rarely discussed his family. He never said much about you." It sounded more like a question than a statement.

"We weren't very close," I said. That statement was in danger of becoming a mantra.

"Still, it must have been a shock finding him like that. You have my deepest sympathy."

I thanked him for his condolences and steered him round to the main purpose of my visit. "It was also a shock to find the police still involved. Have you any idea what's going on?"

Trivett squirmed in his seat. "I'm afraid that may be my fault. I'd better explain. But first I'm sure we could both do with a cup of hot warming tea."

Before I could protest that a cup of hot warming tea was the last thing on my mind, he turned to the doorway and called out, "Sweetheart, I'm sure our guest could use something warm to drink."

Almost immediately, Trivett's 'sweetheart' entered the room carrying a tea tray.

"All ready and waiting," she said.

Her photograph hadn't done her justice. She was a startlingly attractive woman. Soft skinned with radiant azure-blue eyes in a heart-shaped face framed by short dark hair. She sized me up with a bold stare.

A white cotton figure-hugging top with a scooped neck showed off her tan and a whole lot more. She was not at all what I'd expected of a curate's wife. Particularly, one of Trivett's ill-favoured appearance. Shows how easily we allow ourselves to be influenced by stereotypes.

We went through the now usual formalities of introductions and condolences.

Leaning over the coffee table, Frances Trivett played the dutiful housewife and poured our teas, fixing me with a look that was anything but dutiful and wondered with a murmur if she could offer me a biscuit. The tone of voice suggested that more biscuits were on offer but I declined anyway.

All of this play went unnoticed by her dewy-eyed husband. If love truly was blind, then Giles Trivett was living proof.

Frances left us with a backward glance and a teasing smile.

Trivett waited until she had retreated and turned his attention back to me. "Oh, you'll be wanting these." He leaned over to an occasional table by the side of his chair, picked up a set of keys, and handed them to me.

I pocketed them. "You said something about this being your fault," I reminded him, eager for an explanation.

"Ah, yes." He ran a hand over his thinning hair. "When Sgt Lowe dropped off your keys yesterday afternoon, I happened to mention that your father had a visitor the other day. Jonas Wainwright. He's a local builder. It seems your father had asked him to quote for some work."

While I drank my tea, Trivett went on to explain that he had seen Wainwright at the vicarage door and gone out to question him. He had learned that Wainwright's appointment had been two days earlier but that on his arrival, he had heard my father engaged in a violent argument inside. Not wanting to get involved, he had left, intending to speak to my father later in the week. But on his return that day, he had been unable to get a response to his knocking.

"As your father's visitor may have been the last to see him alive," said Trivett, "and there seems to have been some sort of altercation, it obviously raised some concerns and the police must have decided it was worth more scrutiny."

More scrutiny was one thing but to turn what was, for the police, a relatively minor incident into a full-scale criminal investigation on the basis of a recent argument was ludicrous. Unless there was something Trivett and I were unaware of.

"Have you any idea who it was?" I asked.

"Wainwright seemed to think he recognised the voice, but he didn't tell me who."

"Did you hear or see anything?"

"I wasn't here. I was away at a conference. But Frances heard the argument. It was loud enough to carry over here. She didn't recognise the voice though. We told all this to Sgt Lowe yesterday."

I acknowledged what he'd told me but I didn't accept the necessity of a scaled-up investigation quite as readily as he had. Not on the basis of a reported argument. Something didn't ring true. The implication of a full forensic investigation was obvious; my father's home was being treated as a crime scene. And the only crime that fitted the circumstances was murder.

Just as well my next call was to the police station. Sgt Lowe had some explaining to do.

CHAPTER SIX

The desk sergeant dropped the receiver back on the hook. "Sgt Lowe will be with you shortly, Sir. I understand he's been trying to get hold of you all morning." His tone was disapproving.

"Well, I'm here now."

The sergeant didn't look impressed.

I took a seat in the waiting area. A morose-looking youth scowled at me from one of the other metal-framed chairs. He slouched in his seat, hands thrust deep in the pockets of a pair of baggy jeans that had seen better days. Probably someone's Probation Officer.

I was rescued a few minutes later by a fresh-faced young constable who led me down a featureless corridor to an equally featureless interview room. The room was small and windowless. It was oppressive, despite the white-painted walls.

Sgt Lowe was seated at a desk in the centre of the room. He greeted me curtly and waved me towards a chair on the other side of it. The desk was bare but for a recording device sitting between us.

The young constable took up a position in the corner of the room by the door.

Something was out of kilter here. This wasn't the reception I'd expected. There was a change in Lowe's attitude from when we had last met, a coolness.

And then it struck me. I'd sat in on enough police interviews to recognise what this was. I was being treated as a suspect.

"Is this a formal interview?" I asked.

But of course it was. Now that this whole sorry affair had been turned into a criminal investigation, I was the perfect candidate for murderer of the day. Most murders are committed by close family members - though in my case, I'd take issue with the term 'close' - and I was the obvious choice for first in the line of fire.

In his best formal tone, Lowe said, "I'm interviewing you

today in connection with the murder of Owen MacGregor."

So they really were treating my father's death as murder. My mood turned from exasperation to anger. This was so stupid. Bad enough that I had to cope with my father's death in such circumstances and now it was to be investigated as a possible murder because of a presumed argument with someone. It didn't make sense.

I kept my thoughts and my feelings to myself as Sgt Lowe leaned across the table and switched on the recording device. Its baleful red eye gleamed into life and it glared up at me.

Lowe stared directly into my face. No doubt looking for a reaction that would confirm my guilt. I must have been a disappointment to him. It's not as if I didn't know the form and I wasn't about to let him intimidate me.

"Am I under arrest?" I said.

"No, Mr MacGregor. For the moment, this is an interview under caution."

For the moment? That didn't bode well for my prospects. And I knew enough to know that an 'interview under caution' was police speak for 'we know you're as guilty as hell but we can't prove it yet'.

I stared back at him, stony faced, as he advised me of my rights and, for the sake of the recording, registered details of time place and those present.

I was aggrieved. This whole thing seemed such a gross waste of time.

"Look," I said, "I spoke to Trivett this morning. He told me about the argument Jonas Wainwright overheard. It's hardly a justification for turning my father's death into a murder investigation."

"Your father was strangled."

This time, Lowe got a better reaction. My jaw dropped, and I stared back at him, open-mouthed. I trembled as the blood drained from my face. "Strangled?" It came out as a strained whisper. "There has to be some mistake."

"We're still waiting for the Medical Examiner's final report but from the details we already have, there seems little doubt. The deceased had signs of hemorrhaging in the eyes, and contusions and abrasions on the neck. Of course, there will be a full autopsy but we're certain it will confirm what we already know. You father died of manual strangulation."

It didn't make sense. God knows my father could be a difficult man; arrogant, self-opinionated, holier-than-thou. There were many people who had little cause to like him but that was a far cry from wanting to murder him.

"I don't understand. Who would want to do such a thing?"

Stupid question. He didn't need to reply. The answer was in his expression.

"No." I shook my head vigorously. "Don't even go there."

He said, "I'm going to need details of your whereabouts over the last week. And we'll need to contact anyone who can vouch for you."

"Well, that shouldn't be a problem, I spent most of my days at City Road Police Station in London."

"Oh?" He raised an eyebrow.

"Relax, Sergeant. Nothing untoward I assure you. I'm a forensic psychologist. Sometimes, I get asked in to sit in on interviews. It's all in the line of work."

"And the evenings?"

"For God's sake. I live in London. It's miles away."

"It's only two hours by car."

This was unbelievable. "Someone would have seen me if I'd driven down here."

"We're already pursuing that line of enquiry, Sir."

I thought back over the past few days and was instantly relieved. The Gods had blessed me for once. A week earlier and I would have needed to acquaint Sgt Lowe with some of London's lesser known attractions; one or two less than salubrious gay cruising spots and at least one private club that wouldn't be getting its Health and Hygiene certificate any time soon. Fortunately, I'd spent most of my evenings preparing material for my weekly radio broadcast. Alone. In my flat. But, unfortunately, the only evening I could account for was two days before that of the actual broadcast.

"Most of the week, I was at home preparing some work for a radio broadcast," I said. "I host a show on local radio."

"Yes, I've already done some checking. I understand you have a show about investigations into unsolved murders." There was a hint of mockery in his voice. The irony wasn't lost on either of us.

"Among other topics," I said.

"You told me yesterday that you and your father weren't close. Any reason for that?"

"He didn't approve of my lifestyle."

"And was there anything about your lifestyle that warranted that disapproval?"

"My father held strong religious beliefs. I didn't share them."

I cut him off before he could respond. I had no intention of discussing the more personal aspects of my life with the police. It was no one's business but mine.

"I'm not sure where this is going, Sgt Lowe, but if every child murdered his or her father because of disagreements about lifestyle choices, there wouldn't be many surviving parents."

"I suppose that depends on how strongly they disagreed."

Wearied by this line of questioning, I fell back in my chair. "Any disagreements we had were settled twelve years ago. I left Elders Edge and never looked back."

"Until now."

"Until now. And you already know why that is. And let's face it, Sergeant, if I had killed my father, would it make sense to come back to the scene of the crime and draw attention to myself by trying to break down his door?"

Lowe conceded that such an act may well be stupid but pointed out that people often did stupid things.

The interview carried on in this vein for a while. Lowe probed into areas I preferred to avoid; details of my family life, any other close relationships. And I countered by side-stepping any issues I was uncomfortable with.

"What about this visitor my father argued with?" I asked.

"Did Wainwright give you a name?"

"We're pursuing all lines of enquiry, Mr MacGregor. You don't need to concern yourself."

Like hell I didn't. If he wasn't going to pass on any details, I would have to follow up on them myself. It would be easy enough to track down Wainwright. And I had no intention of sitting around while Lowe tried to make a case against me.

After some more questioning, Lowe brought the interview to a close. He made all the usual demands about my needing to let him have contact details and where I could be reached, and making sure I was available for further questioning. As I rose to leave, I confirmed I would be staying at the Fairview for the foreseeable future.

"Someone from Headquarters will want to talk to you," he said. "Now the case has been escalated to a murder investigation, it's being handed over to CID. Detective Chief Inspector Quarryman from Divisional Headquarters in Charwell will be heading the task force."

Another shock. "Not Nathan Quarryman?"

"Yes. You know him?" He grunted. "But I suppose you must. He's a local boy too. Another old friend?" His tone was sarcastic.

The tightness in my throat was back. "Once maybe. A long time ago."

I'd always known Nathan was following in his father's footsteps by joining the force. He was already on his probationary course while we were still together. But I had always presumed, wrongly it seems, that his life and career had eventually taken him away from the county. And now it seems I was going to have to face him after all.

It was ironic that those choices I had made so long ago, that had taken me away from Elders Edge and all my perceived problems, had led me back here, to this time and place, forcing me to confront the very issues I had sought to avoid. Someone once told me that when your chickens come home to roost they often arrive in flocks. How right he was.

CHAPTER SEVEN

Everyone knows everyone in a small town like this. And in particular, everyone knows the local trades people. So tracking down Jonas Wainwright's house was no problem. A rain-soaked postman, taking cover in a nearby bus shelter, was happy to point me in the right direction.

The storm that had threatened for most of the morning now raged overhead. Heavy rain, driven by a howling wind, swept across the road before me in blinding sheets, reducing visibility, and hammering the roof of the Elan like the fists of a vengeful God.

Ahead of me, other vehicles appeared like phantoms out of the storm-light and glided by on wings of water.

The turbulent weather matched the turmoil in my mind; a roiling emotional mix of shock resentment anger anxiety and unease. Shock at discovering the violent nature of my father's death. Resentment and anger at being treated as a potential perpetrator of such a sickening act. And anxiety and unease at learning of Nathan's involvement.

My father had never been an easy man to get along with. But for all his faults he hadn't deserved to end his days like that. I dreaded to think what it must have been like for him. To have stared into the face of his killer as he had the life slowly squeezed from him.

And I was still angry at being thought capable of such an act, fuming at the way I had been treated back at the station. I told myself it was just routine. Nothing personal. It's not as if I hadn't witnessed many such interviews in the past but, somehow, sitting on the other side of that desk, was a whole new experience. It's hard to be objective when you're being treated as a potential murderer.

And then there was Nathan. That had freaked me out.

Once I'd left Elders Edge all those years ago, I'd avoided all Karen's attempts to discuss him. Deliberately put him from my mind. I think she'd secretly hoped we'd get together again. But that bridge had been well and truly burned. Once it was over, it was over, and it would have been futile not to sever all links. Why would I need reminders of happier times? Much too painful. And, because I'd deliberately avoided all discussion of Nathan, I'd always thought that maybe he too had made a fresh start somewhere else.

However, he was unlikely to involve himself in the investigation at a local level. Charwell was twenty miles away. That meant he had a wide jurisdiction and, okay, so murder isn't exactly a minor offence but, even so, he was more likely to leave local matters to the local force and oversee the operation from the Divisional Headquarters at Charwell. So I could breathe easy again. I wasn't likely to run into him any time soon.

By the time I reached Wainwright's place, I was more at ease.

The house was a large detached two-storey affair at the front of The Heights, a private estate off the Charwell Road. Obviously, the down-turn in the building trade over the past few years hadn't reached this far. Or maybe Jonas Wainwright didn't have much competition. Either way, he seemed to have done well for himself.

As impressed as I was with the house, I was less than impressed by the distance between the gate and the house itself. By the time I reached the door, I was drenched.

The woman who answered my ring, didn't even bother to ask who I was. She took one look at me, grabbed my arm, and pulled me out of the rain into a large wood-tiled hallway where I stood dripping onto the floor.

She was a slender woman, not very tall, with an elfin face framed by short wispy blonde hair. She had a duster in one hand and behind her, in the middle of the hall, was a vacuum cleaner. I had interrupted her chores.

"You must be mad coming out in this weather," she said. And then, narrowing her eyes, she added, "And I must be mad letting you in. I hope you're not trying to sell me anything or I'm pushing you straight back out the door."

Faced with a look that could fell a charging rhino at ten paces,

I raised my hands in mock surrender, grateful I'd had the foresight to make the right career choice. "Not guilty."

I introduced myself and suffered the now familiar words of condolence as her expression changed to one of sympathetic concern.

She told me what a shock it had been to learn of my father's death. The news had spread rapidly once the police had started interviewing local people.

"To think that such a thing could happen in a place like this," she said. "And to the local priest. It doesn't bear thinking about. He was such a nice man. I always got on well with your father."

How sincere she was about that was anyone's guess. My father wasn't someone I would describe as 'nice'. But perhaps, given the circumstances, she was being polite.

I thanked her for her kind words and said, "I was hoping to speak to your husband if he's around."

"My husband?" Her forehead creased. And then she smiled and relaxed again. "You mean Jonas. He's not my husband. I'm his domestic help. My name's Erin, Erin Corby." She explained that she cleaned for a number of people in the town. "I worked for your father too."

"So you would have seen him recently?"

"I should have been there last week but he 'phoned and put me off. He wasn't feeling too well."

"Can you remember just when that was?"

"It was last Tuesday. I've already told the police."

I ran over the time-line in my mind. Last Tuesday was five days ago. That would explain why Sgt Lowe wanted to know my whereabouts only over the past week; my father was still alive before then.

It also meant that Erin Colby may have been among the last to speak to my father before he met his murderer.

I was about to ask for Jonas Wainwright's whereabouts when I was interrupted by the sound of a door slamming above us, followed by footsteps crossing the upper floor. I looked up, reacting to the sound.

Erin Corby followed my gaze. "That's Jonas's daughter, Laura. She's doing her homework."

"At least she's supposed to be," she said, raising her voice and turning towards the stairs as the girl stepped down into the hall. "Shouldn't you be working young lady?"

Laura Wainwright must have been in her early teens. She had long blonde hair and blue eyes, and was dressed in a pink-and-white floral-print mini dress that seemed far too sophisticated for a girl of her age. Makeup and a pair of cheap looking earrings in pierced ears completed the look. Maybe I was getting old but I'm sure when I was that age, girls were still girls and didn't try to dress as young adults. Kids were growing up too quickly these days.

I was thinking like my father. The realisation made me shudder.

"I'm hungry," Laura said. "I just wanted a snack."

She disappeared through a door opposite and appeared a minute or two later with a large bag of crisps which she opened and munched from, all the while watching me with open curiosity as I talked with Erin.

I learned from Erin that Jonas Wainwright was working on site all day. Some new development over by Tinkers Wood. Once she'd given me directions, I said my goodbyes and turned to leave.

That's when I saw the bracelet on Laura's wrist.

I recognised it immediately. A triple sapphire fascia set in a gold chain. There wasn't another one like it. It was a present from my father to my mother when they were first married. He'd had it made especially for her. It was unique and very valuable. Quite apart from its monetary value, it was my mother's favourite piece and, after her death, it had acquired a special sentimental value for my father. Not for one moment did I believe he would part with such a precious item.

"That's a nice bracelet, Laura," I said. "Where did you get it?"

She flushed. "I got it down at the market." She clasped a hand over it as if to hide it.

Erin beamed. "She likes her jewellery does Laura. Pity she doesn't like her homework as much." She clapped her hands. "Off you go young lady."

Laura pulled a face and made her way back up the stairs, crunching crisps.

"Do you take Laura with you on your cleaning jobs," I asked Erin.

"Sometimes." She lowered her voice to a conspiratorial whisper and added, "You won't know but her mother died last year. Breast cancer. Laura was devastated. Thirteen is a difficult enough age without having that to deal with too. So I've been happy enough to help out and take her under my wing. She needs a lot of attention at the moment."

"I'm sure Mr Wainwright must be grateful for your help."

She beamed.

I said my goodbyes again, and we parted company.

There was no doubt in my mind that Laura had taken the bracelet during one of her visits to my father's house with Erin Corby. It was inconceivable that she would have acquired it by any other means. But I was going to have to be careful how I dealt with the problem. In the circumstances, it would have been inappropriate to confront Laura directly. Especially in light of the stressful time she'd been through. All the same, it was a problem I was going to have to deal with. I would need to talk to Erin Corby some time soon.

CHAPTER EIGHT

The half-completed new development at the far side of Tinkers Wood was one of those private mock-Georgian estates that seemed to have found favour with the aspiring upper middle classes. It was called 'The Cedars', a pretentious name meant to appeal to its particular customer base.

A tall muscular man in a hard hat was barking orders to a group of five labourers emerging from a Portakabin at the far side of the development. Jonas Wainwright, presumably. He was a big robust bear of a man with a swarthy complexion half hidden by a thick growth of beard. He looked the typical man's man. I couldn't imagine his having to raise a teenage daughter alone. It must be hard on him.

The rain had eased to a fine drizzle and it looked as if the building crew were about to resume work after the sudden downpour. Wainwright saw my approach and walked over to me.

He wiped a hand on his overalls and held it out. "Mr MacGregor?"

We shook hands and he chuckled at my obvious surprise. "Erin called me," he explained. "She said you were on your way."

"Did she tell you why?"

"Some." He placed a hand on my back. "Come, we can talk better inside."

He steered me over to the Portakabin. The metal and canvas chairs inside didn't look particularly comfortable, but I was grateful for the warmth given out by a fan heater by the door. I found a place by the window on one side of a long metal table that ran down the middle of the cabin, and Wainwright sat on the other side of it.

The sound of power tools filtered through to us mixed with the shouted banter of the work crew as they resumed work. Nearby a reversing mechanical digger, in sight of the window, sounded its beeped warning.

Wainwright offered his condolences. I was getting used to the routine by now.

"Your father helped me through a difficult period," he said.

"Yes, I heard you lost your wife. It can't have been an easy time."

"It was breast cancer see. Same as your mother. He told me about that. It helped being able to talk about it with someone who'd been through it too."

I murmured my sympathies.

"My girl too. She was screwed up back then. Kids her age go through enough changes without having to lose their mothers into the bargain."

I had wondered whether I should say something to Wainwright about the bracelet but thought better of it. Perhaps it would be best, after all, to speak to Erin.

I said, "I'm sure Erin must be a great help."

"Your father too. Laura clammed up see. Found it hard to talk about. But he got her to open up. He was good with her. She confided in him."

Jonas was talking about the man who had disowned me all those years ago for daring to go against his values. It was hard to believe we were talking about the same person. And irrational though it was, I resented hearing of his offering comfort and concern to others when his own son, at a time of need, could have benefited from some of that same concern. But in the circumstances, such resentment seemed petty. I pushed all such thoughts aside.

I said, "I spoke to Giles Trivett, my father's curate, earlier. He told me you visited my father recently."

"That's right. I'd been carrying out some minor building repairs at the vicarage and he wanted to discuss some additional work that needed doing. I was always happy to do the odd job for free. It was the least I could do."

"You never got to see him? Is that right?"

Wainwright gripped the edge of the table. "I still can't believe what's happened. The police were round first thing asking questions. I don't suppose you've heard any more?"

"No. The last I heard, the one lead they had was from

information you gave them. You overheard him arguing with someone. They seem to think that might be significant."

Wainwright looked uncomfortable. "That's right."

"Could you tell me who it was?"

He paused and then spoke again more guardedly. "I'm not sure I should. See, at the time I was certain I recognised the voice. But given what happened, well, it makes you wonder doesn't it? I'd hate to think I'd got it wrong and given the police the wrong name."

"I understand your concern, but if I knew who it was, I might be able to throw some light on what it was about. It could have been about something I'd discussed with my father."

I hadn't spoken to my father in weeks but Wainwright wasn't to know that. In fact, I wouldn't even call it speaking. It had been more of a one-sided rant about my latest marital rift.

I continued, "It might even help whoever it was. You may have known my father well enough to realise that he could be an irascible old devil at times. It may all have been innocent and above board."

Wainwright didn't respond immediately. The fan heater whirred and the rain pattered on the roof.

Finally, he said, "I don't suppose it can do any harm. And you're right, it was probably nothing. It was Derek Black. He's a doctor at the local surgery. We saw a lot of him while my wife was having treatment. That's why I thought I recognised his voice. Is that of any help?"

"I know my father wasn't in the best of health but I wasn't aware of any specific problems. He wasn't ill, was he?"

"Not that I know of. I remember Erin said something about him not feeling too well. He put her off coming over. But I got the impression it was just a cold or something."

"It doesn't explain the argument either. Though it wouldn't be unlike my father to contradict his doctor's advice."

"It sounded a bit more serious than that. Quite a violent shouting match. You could hear it out in the courtyard."

"You didn't overhear any of it?"

"No. And I didn't stick around long enough to hear much anyway. I left them to it. I went back two days later. But I couldn't rouse him. He must have already ... you know."

I affirmed my understanding and said, "Which means Dr Black may have been one of the last to see my father."

Wainwright agreed. "I'm sure the police will sort it out with him as soon as they track him down."

"Track him down? They haven't spoken to him yet?"

"I got the impression Dr Black was out of town at the moment."

"Well, maybe they can throw some more light on it over at the surgery."

"I'm sure they can." Wainwright rose from his chair, signalling the end of our conversation and I followed suit.

"Let me know if there's anything I can do to help," he said. "I'd be only too willing."

"Thanks, I will." Before leaving, I said, "I'm glad my father was able to help you."

CHAPTER NINE

What was it with doctors' receptionists? The one at the local surgery was being particularly difficult. Getting past security at MI6 would have been less of a challenge.

She wore a name tag. Holly. Most appropriate. She was as prickly as her namesake.

"It's really not that difficult a request, Holly," I said. "I need to know where I can get hold of Dr Black."

In a tone that could freeze water, she said, "I have no idea where Dr Black is at the moment." She glared at me from the other side of a hatch that divided the reception office from the patients' waiting room.

"And even if I did know," she continued, "I'm not at liberty to give out such information to the general public."

She used the term 'general public' as though describing a lower life form. And then, gripping the edge of the counter with pudgy hands, she pushed herself up to the full extent of her stubby height as if to emphasise the point. Behind her, a typist at a workstation hammered her keyboard with extra vigour and shot me a fierce glance as if to show solidarity with her colleague.

It was time to pull rank. I fished into the inside pocket of my coat, pulled out a calling card, and thrust it in her face. "I'm not a member of the general public. I'm a forensic psychologist. I work with the police." It wasn't exactly a lie. I do work with the police. Just not in this particular instance is all. But she wasn't to know that. "I need to speak with Dr Black as a matter of urgency."

She wrinkled her nose and, in the sort of tone normally adopted for difficult five-year-olds, she said, "I can't tell you any more than our Practice Manager has already told the police."

"And what was that?"

"That Dr Black is out of town visiting family. And we don't know when he'll be back."

"When did he leave?"

"A week ago."

That would be around the time he visited my father. Perhaps

there was a connection."

"And you didn't think to ask when he'd be back?"

She bristled. "He left an answer-phone message. It was some sort of family emergency. He didn't say when he would be back and he's not been in touch since."

"Do you know where he can be contacted? Do you have any addresses or phone numbers for his family?"

"I'm not privy to that sort of information. And besides you should have it already. Our Practice Manager has already passed on all Dr Black's personal details. They should be on your records."

She sounded suspicious. Time to try a different approach. "Perhaps I should have a word with your Practice Manager. I have some more questions I'd like to ask."

Holly's voice was getting squeakier by the minute. "She is rather busy."

"I'm sure she wouldn't want to hinder the police investigation unduly. Please tell her I'd like to see her."

I was rewarded with a look that could sour wine as she reached for the telephone on the counter. She turned her back on me, made the call, and spoke into the receiver in a hushed tone. I overheard her say that someone from the police was waiting in reception. I pretended not to hear.

"She's sending someone out for you," Holly said, replacing the receiver. She sounded glad to be getting rid of me.

A younger woman appeared from a door across the room and greeted me with a smile - obviously not a receptionist - and led me to a nearby office where she left me in the company of the Practice Manager who rose from behind her desk as I entered. She introduced herself as Marion Porter.

After offering me a seat, Ms Porter said, "I'm a little puzzled. I've already given you as much information as I have. I don't know what else I can help you with."

She resumed her seat and, hands clasped before her on the desk, waited for an explanation.

She was a formidable looking woman, unsmiling, brisk and to

the point, the no-nonsense type who wouldn't suffer fools gladly.

Sweat dampened my forehead. I'd missed some opportunities to correct the assumption that I was working with the police in their search for Dr Black. I hadn't actually said I was but the failure to correct the assumption was as much a deception. And Marion Porter didn't strike me as the kind of woman to be easily hoodwinked for long. Time to extricate myself. Clearly, I wasn't going to get the information I wanted.

I said, "I wanted to satisfy myself on a point regarding the call itself. Could you tell me how Dr Black sounded? Did he sound distressed or upset?"

"Ah." She leaned back in her chair and clasped her hands together. "Perhaps I didn't make it clear. Dr Black left an automated text message. So I can't tell you how he sounded."

"A text message? That seems strange. Why would he not call in person or leave a voice message? It surely would have been easier?"

"I can't answer that. But it would make sense if he was in a situation where he didn't want to be overheard."

"I guess so."

I'd come to a dead end.

CHAPTER TEN

Karen was leaning over the reception desk browsing through the register when I returned. I reached behind me with a foot and kicked the door shut against the buffeting wind. It slammed into its frame and Karen looked up abruptly, peering over the top of her reading spectacles.

"Where the hell have you been all day?" She took off her specs and put them on the counter. "Have you any idea what's been going on?"

"Sure." I hung my wet coat on the stand by the door. "My father's been murdered and I'm the number one suspect."

"What?" She closed the register with a thud. "Oh, Mikey, that's insane."

"Try telling that to your boyfriend."

I crossed over to the fire and stood with my back to the flames. The spreading warmth was slow to ease the aching cold in my bones. Or take the edge off my temper. I was still aggrieved at failing to obtain any useful information at the surgery.

Karen came over to join me. "He is not my boyfriend. We're just friends. And I don't suppose for one moment he thinks you're a suspect."

"He just spent the morning interrogating me and I didn't get the impression he wanted to bond."

"Of course he's going to question you. You're Owen's closest family. And you found the body. What did you expect?"

I grunted and rubbed the back of my neck, easing the tension in the muscles there. Karen was right of course. I was being unreasonable. Lowe was doing his job and his cross-examination was just part of the routine.

I pulled a face. "Sorry, I'm being a jerk. Ignore me. It's been one of those days."

Karen squeezed my arm. "It must have been such a shock. I still can't believe it. Who would want to do such a thing?"

"Well, I've already told you what your ... what Sgt Lowe

thinks. My dysfunctional relationship with my father seemed to be of particular interest to him."

"And what did you tell him?"

"As little as possible."

I didn't need to elaborate. Karen was close enough to know the many problems I'd had with my father.

"Come on," she said. "Let's get ourselves a drink. I think you need one. Sounds like you're having a bad time."

She led the way through an archway on the far side of the reception area and into the bar. "I may have closed down for the winter but I always keep a bottle of my favourite scotch handy."

I pulled a stool up to the counter and seated myself. Karen reached over and produced a bottle of Glenfiddich and some glasses. She slid onto the stool next to me and treated us both to a large measure. A couple of shots later I was more amiable.

Now I was in a better frame of mind, I told her about my day so far, including my visits to Jonas and the surgery.

I saved the best till last. "You're not going to believe who's in charge of the investigation."

"Ah, yes, I was just about to tell you."

There was something about the way she said it that made me wary. "What is it?"

She bit her lip. "Nathan phoned. He wants to speak to you."

I groaned. My sense of wellbeing was dissipating again.

"I hope you put him off."

"For God's sake, Mikey. It wasn't a social call. He's running a murder investigation."

I slouched over the bar. "I was hoping I wouldn't have to face him."

"Well it's high time you did. You need to start facing up to your responsibilities and stop being such a coward."

I shot upright again. A coward? That was a kick in the teeth. "Is that what you think? That I'm a coward?"

She stared at me for a long moment and then said, "I know what a difficult time it was for you, Mikey. And I know how hard it was to leave everything behind. But it wasn't just about you, was it? You were in a relationship."

"And you'd know all about relationships. Yours was such a huge success."

That was wrong, so wrong. I leaned on the bar-top, buried my face in my hands and groaned. "I'm so sorry, Karen. That was a rotten thing to say. I'm sorry."

The wind howled in the chimney, sending a shower of soot into the blazing hearth below. The fire spluttered and flared.

Karen said, "My ex gave me good reason to leave him." Her tone had cooled. "What reason did Nathan give you?"

I didn't answer. I really should learn to think before I opened my mouth.

"You have no idea how much you hurt him. And I was the one left behind to pick up the pieces. And for all these years, you refused to talk about it and I let you get away with it. Well, it's time you knew."

This was unexpected.

"Yes, Mikey, you're a coward. What you did, the way you treated him, was contemptible."

I should have tried to defend myself but I was too stunned. Is that what she really thought, had always thought?

The ensuing silence was broken by the plaintive sound of the wind.

Karen slid off the stool and made her way back to the reception area. "He's coming round this evening at six. Make sure you're here."

She left the room and closed the door behind her.

CHAPTER ELEVEN

Back in my room, I pulled a chair over to the window and sat facing the sea.

The wind had increased in force and was blowing in behind the waves, lifting them high over the seawall to crash down onto the Esplanade below. Seawater swept across the road and lashed the sides of passing vehicles.

As the scene slowly faded into growing darkness, my thoughts strayed to the past.

Once I'd made that fateful decision to leave Elders Edge all those years ago, I never saw Nathan again. Never contacted him. Never told him of my plans. But was that cowardice? I didn't think so. It was the hardest thing I've done. If I'd faced him then, I would have crumbled, my resolve shattered. And so I walked away and tried to forget him. And over time, my remembrance of him became a dull ache that I pushed to the back of my mind. I'd tried so hard not to think about him and now he was about to walk back into my life. And for the first time in many years, I would be forced to confront all those unanswered questions I'd shied away from; how life had been for him, if he blamed me for the choices I'd made and, if so, if he had learned to forgive me.

For the rest of that afternoon, I wandered around my room, unable to settle to anything, my mind in overdrive.

About an hour before Nathan was due to arrive, I ran a bath and took a long leisurely soak, trying to relax. But without success.

I finished my bath and dressed, going for my usual casual style; a dark-blue Lacoste polo shirt, a pair of Hugo Boss Alabama jeans and Nike trainers.

Just before he was due to arrive, I checked my reflection in the mirror. Not too bad. I looked a bit tired, but I'd pass muster.

Down below the outer door slammed. The sound of voices drifted up, Karen's and a deeper rumbling bass. My watch told me it was six o'clock. It had to be him. He had always been a stickler for punctuality.

CHAPTER TWELVE

On the upper landing, I gripped the bannister rail and willed my muscles to relax. A tight hard knot formed in my stomach.

For the past few hours, I'd run through all manner of different scenarios in my mind, agonising over the many possible ways this meeting could pan out. None of them good. I had no real idea what to expect, but it wasn't going to be a pleasure ride.

I stood there long enough to compose myself, and then made my way down to reception, determined to appear at ease, even if I didn't feel it.

He was seated by the fire and rose to face me as I reached the foot of the stairs. Karen had already made herself scarce.

The years had been good to him. A few extra crinkles around the eyes maybe and the close-cropped smoky-brown hair was greying at the temples. But he was still the tall handsome man I remembered; the dark brooding good looks and those molten green eyes that seemed to burn into you.

We faced each other across the room in silence like gunslingers at a duel, each waiting for the other to make the first move. He was sizing me up and, under that unflinching gaze, I felt exposed and vulnerable.

Behind him, a blazing fire crackled in the grate.

Trying to brazen it out with a smile, I said, "Hello, Nathan. It's good to see you."

"Mikey." His response was as curt as the nod that accompanied it. The solid square-jawed face remained expressionless.

He never had been much of a talker. No point wasting words when a nod or a frown or a grunt would do.

I tried again. "You're looking well."

He was too. And obviously still making good use of the gym. There was no hiding the taut firm muscles that strained against the white cotton shirt. And although he had filled out a bit, the few extra pounds looked good on his tall well-proportioned frame.

I didn't know what else to say, all the carefully rehearsed words forgotten. There was so much I wanted to explain. But I didn't know how.

Needing to say something, anything, I added, "I always meant to get in touch." I regretted the words as soon as they were out of my mouth. They sounded so lame. And we both must have known it was a lie.

The muscles in his jaw tensed momentarily but instead of responding directly, he said instead, "I'm sure you know why I'm here. I'm sorry for your loss."

Still flustered by my tactlessness and without thinking, I said, "I doubt that," and immediately flushed. "I'm sorry. That was dumb."

This was not going well. He'd had no cause to like my father any more than I had. And he knew there was no love lost between us. But still, it was a cheap shot in the circumstances.

He let the moment pass and said, "I wanted to introduce myself as the senior officer in charge of the investigation into your father's death."

I stiffened. Introduce himself? What was he saying? He spoke as though he was meeting me for the first time. Who did he think I was?

For the next few minutes, I listened, bemused, while he explained how the investigation had been handed over from the local force to Divisional Headquarters in Charwell and that he would be taking a personal interest in the case.

In a neutral professional tone, he outlined the course the investigation was taking, including house to house enquiries and the interviewing of friends, family, colleagues and anyone else who had regular and even casual contact with my father. He explained that I would, of course, be included in that list of interviewees and he would be following up on my interview with Sgt Lowe.

I was confused.

Here was the man I had known for most of my life, from the earliest days of our childhood, and he addressed me as if he were briefing a potential witness on first acquaintance. The impassioned outburst I had expected wasn't forthcoming. Instead, what I got was this cool formality. A salesman trying to sell me a new car would have shown more emotion.

He continued, "I like to work in the field sometimes. I like my men to know that I'm prepared to work alongside them. It's good for morale."

I searched his face as he spoke. Looked for the person I had once known. The one who had loved me and held me in his arms. But he wasn't there. Just this solemn stranger.

An emotional confrontation had been the last thing I'd wanted. But now I almost wished there had been one. Anything would have been better than this.

"There is one matter I need to raise with you," he said. "I had a call from the local surgery. I understand you've been making some enquires of your own."

"I couldn't stand by and do nothing."

"The staff there were under the mistaken impression you were interviewing them on behalf of the police. I can't imagine how they could have arrived at such a conclusion. Can you, Mikey?"

I mumbled something about how easy it was to jump to conclusions.

"Leave it to the police would you. I don't appreciate outside interference."

Outside interference? He'd done it again. Distanced himself. Is that who I was now? An outsider?

"I'm not totally without some experience in the field," I said, trying to keep the resentment out of my voice. "I have been known to be of some value to the police in the past."

His mouth twisted into a sardonic smile. The first hint of emotion I'd seen. "So I hear," he said. "You seem to have made quite a name for yourself over the past few years."

Was that disapproval in his tone?

I said, "A name made on the basis of the expert professional advice I've been able to give to the police on many occasions."

"And which has brought you a lot of media attention that can't have done your bank balance any harm."

What was his problem? Was he deliberately trying to rile me?

"I'll admit I've made a comfortable living out of my media work. But then people are interested in that sort of thing."

"Yes, I've caught one or two of your shows over the years. Though I have to say, your views on some of the more notorious unsolved crimes seem a little fanciful to my mind. I suggest you leave real investigation to those of us who know what we're doing."

So that was it. Professional jealousy. I was stepping on his toes and he didn't like it. Several responses came to mind, none of them particularly constructive. So I bit back my words and changed the subject instead.

"And where do we go from here?" I asked.

"I'll need to speak to you more formally down at the station. But that can wait until tomorrow."

More formally? That was a joke. It got more formal than this?

He said, "I'd like you to be at the station at nine if that's convenient. I can send a car for you if you need one."

"I can make my own way thanks."

"As you wish." He said his goodbyes and headed towards the door.

"Is there nothing else?" Was he going to walk away without a word about everything that had passed between us?

He faced me with a blank stare. "There was something you wanted to discuss?"

I considered this for a moment. And decided that maybe it was best to let it go. "Nothing, I guess."

"Then I'll leave you to enjoy the rest of your evening."

He closed the door behind him and left me standing in the middle of the reception area. Was that it? Was this what it had come down to? This cold indifference. I'd expected something more, some show of emotion. Anger maybe. A demand for an explanation, emotional restitution. And yet it had been that kind of emotional outburst that I had most wanted to avoid. So why was I feeling like this? Why was I so disappointed?

CHAPTER THIRTEEN

There was a reporter from the local press waiting for me outside the police station the following morning. He introduced himself as the crime correspondent for the Charwell Sentinel.

"Jeff Stokes is the name." He held out a hand.

I ignored it. Reporters aren't among my favourite people. Public figures, even minor ones like me, attract the likes of this man, always on the lookout for salacious gossip they can pass on to their readers. I still hadn't forgotten the rough ride I got after the breakup of my first marriage.

"What can I do for you, Mr Stokes?"

The weather hadn't improved much. The rain had stopped but there was still a chill wind blowing in from the sea and I didn't feel like standing around in the cold for the benefit of Mr Stokes.

"Jeff, please," he said, with that phony bonhomie so often adopted by his type. "I was hoping to have a chat about your father's unfortunate death. Get some insights from the point of view of the grieving son. That sort of thing."

"I'm sure you'll appreciate that this is a very difficult time for me, Mr Stokes. And I don't feel ready to talk about my feelings yet."

"Of course, I understand. But maybe one or two quotes. It's going to be our lead story tonight - we're trying to get something out before it hits the Nationals - and a comment or two from you would be appreciated." He reached into a satchel he carried over his shoulder and took out a notebook and pen.

It hadn't occurred to me until that moment that the story of my father's murder would attract a lot of media attention. But of course it was bound to. More aggravation to deal with.

"Then you can say that I was stunned by the news of his death. My father was a peace-loving and well-respected local figure and his murder is as inexplicable as it is shocking."

"And I understand you've been helping the police with their enquires. Anything to say about that?"

I snorted. "I think we both know what is implied by the use of that particular phrase. But I'm sorry to disappoint you. The police just wanted some background information."

"I believe it was you who found the body?"

"That's right."

"Were you alone?"

"No."

What would he have made of it if I had been? I could picture it now. Local priest found strangled after lone visit from well-known son. No need to risk a libel by making a direct accusation. The implication would be obvious. Something for the gossips to mull over.

I said, "I was accompanied by Sgt Lowe of the local police."

"Do you know if the police have any suspects yet?"

"Not that I know of. And now if you'll forgive me, Mr Stokes, I have an appointment in the station. I must go."

"More enquiries?"

"I'm eager to do everything I can to assist the police in helping to find my father's murderer." I cut him short before he could ask any more questions. "And now if you'll excuse me."

I left him standing at the entrance to the station, scribbling in his notebook.

CHAPTER FOURTEEN

Nathan glanced at his watch as I entered his office. He was seated at his desk, an open file in front of him.

"I thought we said nine," he said.

"Sorry, I was waylaid by a reporter from the local paper. He's hanging around outside."

For God's sake, it was only five minutes. I'd forgotten what a pain he could be about punctuality. I pulled back the chair on the other side of the desk and sat down.

"That could be useful," he said.

"Useful?"

"You have a public profile. You attract media attention. When we have no leads, it can be productive to bring this sort of crime to public attention."

"I'm not sure I want the media digging into my private life. And they will. It wouldn't be the first time."

"That's inevitable to some extent. Publicity is a two-edged sword."

"Oh, great. Something to look forward to."

"Of course, if you have nothing to hide..."

I ignored the remark. "If you have no real leads, does that mean I'm off the hook? I think your Sgt Lowe had me down as the prime suspect."

"I'm sure I can vouch for you."

That was some relief at least. "What about this local guy? Dr Black? Any luck there?"

"He has a daughter in Sheffield. The local force are making enquires. We should hear from them shortly."

He rocked back in his chair and steepled his fingers. "But let's get back to you shall we? I need to verify your whereabouts over the last week or so."

There was a sinking feeling in my stomach. No way was I going to discuss the intimate details of my private life with Nathan Quarryman of all people.

"I gave all this information to Sgt Lowe. What else can I tell you?"

He leaned forward, rifled through the file, and stopped at a page about halfway through. "You say here you were alone in your flat for most of the week. I understand you married again a few years ago. And yet there's no mention of your wife as an alibi."

"I thought you said I was off the hook here. This sounds very much like an interrogation to me."

His expression hardened and he fixed me with a look that dared me to question him. "You know the score, Mikey. You've been involved in enough investigations to know how it works. We do this by the numbers."

"It feels very different when you're on the other side of an investigation."

"I'm sure it does." He leaned back in his chair. "So, what's the score here?"

As far as I was concerned, my marital problems were my business. Not something to be pawed over in public.

"I have my own flat in the city where I do most of my work. I like to be alone. It helps me concentrate. I was there all week."

"Well that takes care of the past week. What about the week before?"

My throat tightened. I knitted my brows as if trying to recollect. "I can't be sure." I was trying to think fast, find some sort of explanation that would sound reasonable.

"It was just a week ago."

"I lead a busy life. What can I say?"

His pinched expression suggested he wasn't too happy about my casual dismissal of his questioning. I had to come up with something but decided to leave out the parts about my more nefarious activities. Perhaps a nod in the direction of the truth might help.

"Look," I said, "I really have been spending more time alone recently."

I paused, a moment of discomfort, and then continued. "My wife and I are going through a difficult patch and I've been staying in my flat for the past few weeks. So, you see, I can't use her as an alibi."

He stared at me without speaking and then picked up a pen and scribbled something in his file.

I squirmed in my chair. Nathan Quarryman was the last person I wanted to discuss my marital rift with but at least it got me off the hook.

He continued pressing me for more information. Places I had been. People who might be able to give me an alibi. I countered as best I could, giving details of my more mundane activities including visits to my agent, and time spent in the research department of the local library. For the rest, I claimed to have been alone in my flat. Which was certainly true for some of the time.

Finally, he closed the file and straightened it. I could only hope he was satisfied with my answers.

"Let me know if you think of anything else," he said.

"Sure I will."

Like hell I would. What I got up to in my private life was not something I wanted leaking to press. And it's that sort of information that somehow managed to get out.

"And one more thing, Mikey. I don't want you getting involved in the investigation. Leave the interviewing to us."

I opened my mouth to protest.

He cut me off. "No. I know what you're going to say and I appreciate you have some relevant expertise. But you're personally involved in this case and it may not be appropriate to take part in the investigation."

If he remembered anything about me at all, he would know I wasn't about to take a damn bit of notice. Of course I was going to involve myself.

"There is one matter I need to deal with," I said.

I explained about my visit to Jonas Wainwright's place and seeing my mother's bracelet on Laura Wainwright's wrist.

"It's a very expensive piece of jewellery," I said. "And I can't believe Laura Wainwright got it through legitimate means."

"You don't want the police involved?" Nathan asked.

"Hardly. She's just a kid. And she's had a rough time of it. Her mother died last year and she's not coping too well. I think it's best if I have a quiet word with Erin."

"Okay. Do you have her address?"

"No. Not yet."

"I'll get the Desk Sergeant to look it up for you. But no more than that, you understand?"

I kept silent.

"I think that's it for the moment then. But get back to me if there's anything else you can think of."

He rose in anticipation of finishing the interview. I stayed in my seat.

"There is something else I'd like to talk about," I said. "A personal matter."

His brow wrinkled. He seemed genuinely puzzled and sat down again, waited for an explanation.

Did he think there was nothing to say? This was going to be embarrassing but I needed to clear the air.

"I want to talk about us."

"Us?"

"Oh, please, Nathan. You know what I mean. Since my return, you've treated me like a stranger, as if nothing happened between us. We have a history."

"One that ended very abruptly as I remember. Your choice. What do you want from me, Mikey?"

"It didn't end well. Maybe I'm looking for closure."

"Closure?" He raised an eyebrow and snorted. "You got all the closure you needed. You walked away."

"And you have nothing to say about that?"

He leaned toward me, arms on the desk. "Look, Mikey, you made your choice a long time ago. What's done is done. You moved on. You have a wife and a different life now. And I had to move on too. Let's just leave it at that, shall we?"

"I wanted to explain. Tell you how and why."

"The time for explanations is long gone. Let it be."

"Can't we still be friends?"

His jaw tightened, and I caught the glimpse of some fleeting emotion cross his face. Anger? I couldn't be sure what it was. But when he spoke again, his tone was cool.

"I see no reason why we can't have an amicable working relationship," he said, stiffly.

So that was it. Closure of a sort I guess. It would have to do.

CHAPTER FIFTEEN

Interrupting Erin Colby's chores was becoming a habit. When I arrived, she was standing by her front door shaking the dust from a rug. I crunched my way up the gravel path towards the house and, as I reached the adjoining garage, I was treated to a high octane stream of invective from behind the half-opened doors. Someone was decidedly not in their happy zone.

Reacting to the sudden outburst, Erin looked up and caught sight of my approach. She seemed surprised to see me but greeted me, all the same, with a wave, and then pulled a face.

"That's my husband, Adam", she called out. "Don't mind him. He thinks the car will run better if he abuses it."

In response to Erin's voice, the garage doors were pushed fully open and out stepped a wiry-framed man of average height clad in a blue oil-stained boiler-suit.

He had a firm square face that sported a wide embarrassed grin beneath a prominent nose. Short brick-brown hair, damp with sweat, stuck to his forehead. Thick brows framed silver-grey eyes that caught his smile and twinkled.

" Sorry about that," he said.

Erin introduced us.

Adam Corby adopted a more solicitous demeanour and commiserated with me, expressing his abhorrence at recent events and offering his sympathies for my recent loss.

I accepted his condolences.

He held up his grease-stained hands and said, "I won't shake. I'm in the middle of trying to get this heap of scrap metal back on the road."

Inside the garage was a white Fiat Punto which looked as if it had seen better times. An orange sticker in the back window read 'My other car is a Rolls Royce'. It begged the question why he would want to drive this one.

"I'll leave you to it then," I said. "I wanted a word with Erin."

He raised a hand in acknowledgement and stepped back into the garage.

Erin led the way into the house and through to the living room. She was full of questions about the police investigation, eager for information, and seemed disappointed when I had nothing to tell her.

"There's something else I need to talk to you about," I said. "It's a rather delicate matter."

Picking my words carefully, I told her of my concerns about the bracelet Laura had been wearing and, as I did so, her face slowly crumpled.

"Please don't think I'm accusing her of anything," I said hastily, not wanting to appear too confrontational, "but I find it difficult to believe that my father would have given it to her."

Needing to explain further, I added, "It was my mother's favourite piece of jewellery and I'm sure he wouldn't think of parting with it. Besides which, it's a unique piece and very valuable. Not something you'd give to a young girl. And when Laura said she'd got it from the market, I knew that couldn't be true."

I finished what I had to say and waited for the inevitable barrage of angry denials. It didn't happen.

Instead, Erin sank into a chair and ran a despairing hand through her hair.

"I'm so sorry," she said.

This wasn't what I'd expected.

I seated myself opposite her. "Forgive me for saying so but you don't seem particularly surprised."

"No." She looked drained.

A few moments passed in silence while she composed herself.

She said, "It's not the first time." A pause. "Look, she's been through a bad spell. And this isn't like her. It was after her mother died. That's when it all started."

"I did wonder."

"She took some CDs from one of the other houses I clean. I caught her at it that time and made her put them back. But I found some of my own jewellery in her bedroom when I was cleaning for her dad. Seems she'd been making a habit of it."

"That must have put you in a very awkward position," I said.

"What do you want to do about it?" she asked. "Will you tell the police?"

"I don't think so. I was hoping you might intervene on my behalf. She's had a hard enough time without any more problems."

Erin thanked me profusely. She seemed relieved.

I said. "I'm not saying she should be allowed to get away with it entirely. She needs to know that her behaviour is unacceptable. And if she doesn't change it, there will be consequences."

"Don't you worry about that. I'll make damn sure she doesn't forget about it in a hurry. And I'll be finding her plenty of work to keep her out of trouble."

"Good. Then I'll leave it in your capable hands. And perhaps you can find a way to get the bracelet back to me sometime. I'm staying over at the Fairview on the Esplanade. You know it?"

"Yes, of course." She promised to return the bracelet as soon as possible.

Satisfied with the outcome, I said my goodbyes and took my leave. At least that was one tricky situation easily resolved. For the moment.

CHAPTER SIXTEEN

Jeff Stokes had been true to his word. My father's murder was headline news in the local paper. And it hadn't made just the front page; it had taken over the whole edition. As if details of the murder itself weren't enough, there was also a two page spread devoted to my personal history. Seems like I'd finally made it as man of the month.

Karen was in panic mode. She'd already had calls from several national newspapers checking on room availability. It looked as if they'd be settling in for the long haul. All I needed.

We were seated by the fireside in the Fairview. The evening paper had just been delivered and I was scanning it for the more salacious bits.

Karen was fretting about her staffing problems.

"What am I supposed to do?" she asked. "I use casual staff in the season. It's too late to get anyone now and I don't think I cope with more than one or two guests at this time of year."

"You're not obliged to fix them up with rooms. Let them camp out in the rain somewhere. They're reporters after all. Their thick skins should protect them against the weather."

"Mikey. What's the point of alienating them? How is that going to help?"

I ignored the criticism and continued looking through the paper.

Karen said, "I wonder if I can get some of my summer staff to cover for a while."

I groaned. "Listen to this. Well-loved local priest, Owen MacGregor, was found strangled following a visit from his estranged son, Michael MacGregor, the celebrity radio presenter. Dear God. Why don't they just accuse me of murder and have done with it?"

I flipped through the pages. "At least they haven't got wind of my break up with Donna yet. That's something to be thankful for I guess."

Karen rose from her chair and went over to the reception desk.

"I'm going to ring round and see what I can do about getting some temporary staff."

She delved into a drawer under the desk and produced a battered address book. "If we're going to be swamped by reporters, I'm going to need all the help I can get."

"Christ. I hope it doesn't come to that. The last thing we need is a media circus coming to town."

"In your dreams." She pulled the desk phone towards her and picked up the receiver.

While Karen made her calls, I checked the paper to see if the press had picked up on any negative aspects of my personal life. I was relieved to see I was in the clear. So far.

While I was scrutinising the reported details of my biography and separating fact from fiction, the outer door opened. If it was another reporter, I was out of there. I wasn't in the mood for yet another sycophantic lets-be-friends busybody delving into my private life.

It was Nathan.

He was suited and booted - a dark-grey flannel suit with a white shirt and sober red-and-grey striped tie - so I guessed he was on his way back from the local station.

His open raincoat was wet and he stamped on the floor to shake the rain from his shoes.

I wasn't sure how to deal with him after the way our last meeting had ended. A hearty hail-and-well-met greeting didn't seem appropriate somehow. So I waited for him to speak first.

Karen put down the phone and called out to him from behind the desk, "Hey. How's my second favourite policeman?" She crossed towards him.

He smiled, took her in his arms, and hugged her close. "So, I've been demoted, eh? That's the last time I introduce you to one of my men."

She laughed, pulled away and slow-punched his arm. "Too late now," she said.

It was the first time I'd seen him smile that way since we'd renewed our acquaintance. This was the old Nathan. The easy-going one. The one who enjoyed light-hearted banter with friends. I'd forgotten how his cheek dimpled on one side when he smiled. And the way he held you when he took you in his arms. I turned away unable to look.

"Mikey." The warmth had gone from his voice.

I looked up again. "I take it this isn't a social call. So I presume you have some news for me."

Karen interrupted. "I'll leave you two to talk. I'll be in the back office. Give me a shout before you leave, Nathan."

He smiled at her again and she departed, leaving us together.

"You may as well take a seat," I said. "You can dry out while you talk."

He sat in the armchair on the other side of the hearth and unbuttoned his jacket.

"I won't keep you too long," he said. "I wanted to bring you up to date. We've got some feedback from the South Yorkshire force about Black's family. His daughter hasn't heard from him. And, apparently, they haven't been on speaking terms for years. He doesn't have any other family so his message appears to have been a lie." He must have caught my puzzled look. "What?"

"Just seems strange, that's all. If he's going to lie, why not come up with something that isn't so easily disproved?"

"In my experience, people don't always think these things through."

"Maybe. So what happens now?"

"We put out a call for Black. We need to find him as soon as possible. He's now our prime suspect for your father's murder. Which is why ..." He paused for a moment, and I knew bad news was on the way. "... I'm calling a press conference for tomorrow."

I voiced my objections. "Have you seen the evening paper? Have you seen how they're handling it? You'd think murder was sensational enough without the need for embellishments."

"You're well-known enough for the investigation to get a lot of national coverage. And the sooner that happens, the sooner the public will be on the lookout for Black."

I didn't respond. Much as I hated to admit it, he was right.

"And besides" he said, "once we get attention focused on Black, it takes the heat off you. That can't be a bad thing can it?"

"You wouldn't like to take any bets on that would you?"

"We've already had enquiries from the media. And the BBC are sending a crew down in the morning. We might as well make good use of them."

He rose to leave. "The conference is set for one. So have an early lunch and I'll send a car round for you. Best not to drive in yourself while the press are here."

He called out to Karen as he headed for the door and she appeared from the back office.

"Are you off duty now?" she asked.

"Yes, I'm on my way home."

"In that case why don't you join us for some supper first. It's a long drive back to Charwell."

He shot me a backward glance. "It's best if I don't. I'll catch up with you later," he said. And was gone.

CHAPTER SEVENTEEN

I was glad of the lift to the police station the following day.

A group of media hacks were already there, huddled beneath the canopy at the main entrance, sheltering from the light drizzle. Most of them were chewing the cud or taking the opportunity to enjoy a last cigarette before going inside. A camera crew were setting up their equipment on the forecourt.

I slouched down in my seat to avoid being seen, much to the amusement of my driver, and we drove around to the restricted compound behind the station.

Nathan met us there and briefed me on how the conference would be conducted. He would address the Press, give them a progress report of the investigation so far - not that there was much to tell - and ask for their help in locating Black.

For the moment, Black wouldn't be identified as a suspect but as someone who may have been one of the last to see my father alive and who might have valuable information. Though the Press would make their own assumptions anyway. Then they would be invited to ask questions. That's where I came in.

Nathan said, "Whatever they ask, just stick to what you know. They'll try to get you to speculate about motive and possible suspects, but hold firm. If they get too heavy, I'll intervene."

I accepted his advice and Nathan led the way into the meeting room. My stomach churned and my throat was dry. The sooner this was over, the better.

Elders Edge Police Station was an old Victorian conversion with a modern glass and metal extension built onto the front to make it more attractive to visitors. This room, however, was a large one at the back of the old building. It looked as if it might once have been a factory. Built more for function than aesthetic appeal, it was stark and oppressive. Rows of small windows were set high up around each wall and exposed pipes ran up to the ceiling in three corners. Two larger windows opposite the door looked out onto the courtyard behind the building. Everything was painted white to brighten the room, a failed attempt to make it more appealing.

Cameras clicked as I followed Nathan to a row of three metal-framed chairs against the wall to the left of the door and a murmur ran around the room. Sgt Lowe was already seated in one of the three chairs and a middle-aged stern-looking woman with scraped back hair sat in a separate seat nearby, a notebook in her lap. Nathan took his place in the centre seat and I sat down on the other side of him.

Four rows of metal-framed chairs faced us. Obviously set up especially for this conference. They were filled by members of the Press, some of whom I recognised from earlier encounters. I tried to look as if I was pleased to see them.

Nathan leaned over and spoke with Lowe in a whisper and then turned back, looked around the room, and seemingly satisfied that everyone was ready, called the conference to order.

He addressed the waiting members of the Press, thanked them for coming and told them of the circumstances of the investigation.

He said. "At the moment, we have no suspects but there are a number of people we need to interview."

He told them of Black's involvement and that a search was underway to establish his whereabouts.

"We're going to need your help in finding him. Any information members of the public can give us will be invaluable."

He fed them some details about the medical examiner's report which confirmed that my father had been strangled and then opened the floor to questions.

A young reporter asked. "Is Black a suspect?"

Nathan said, "No, not at the moment. But we do believe he can give us vital information which will help our enquires."

"And what about Mr MacGregor there? Is he a suspect?"

A ripple of laughter went around the room. I opened my mouth to protest but Nathan took control of the exchange. "Mr MacGregor is not a suspect in this case." He spoke in his usual moderate tone, as professional as ever.

"But it was you who found the body wasn't it, Mikey?" This shouted out from the back of the room.

"Sgt Lowe here ... ," I tilted my head towards Lowe, "... was with me. We found the body together." That was one avenue of idle speculation closed off.

Another reporter. This one I recognised. John Chesterton from the Daily Echo. A hardened hack and a major slime-ball if ever there was one. "You don't live down here, Mikey?"

"Not any more, no. I've lived in London for the past twelve years."

Chesterton again. "What brought you down here? Just visiting? I see you didn't bring your family with you."

I couldn't see where he was going with this. Was this leading up to speculation about my relationship with my father? I had to stop him. "It was meant to be no more than a brief visit. A friend who lives locally raised concerns about my father's whereabouts and naturally I was worried about him. I drove down to check up on him."

"So what now? Will you be staying down here?"

"I'll be here for the foreseeable future. Sorting out my father's estate may take a while."

John Chesterton again. "Will your wife be joining you?"

Too late I saw what he was leading up to. He knew about the breakup of my marriage. How much he knew was anyone's guess. I hoped my solicitor had managed to persuade Donna about the need for discretion in the private affairs of those in the public eye.

"I don't see how this is relevant, Mr Chesterton. Perhaps we should stick to the facts of the investigation itself."

He wasn't to be dissuaded. "Is it not the case that you and your wife recently separated following your affair with another man?"

My chest tightened. Clearly, my solicitor's powers of persuasion were sadly lacking.

The room sat in silence, waiting for a response. A draught found its way in through one of the windows and rattled the metal blind.

"May I remind you," I said, "that this press conference was called to ask for your help in finding my father's murderer. In the circumstances, speculation about my private life is neither helpful nor appropriate."

"You're a public figure. The public are going to want to know."

"I've given you the only response you're getting."

"Isn't it also true you've had a number of liaisons with other men during the course of your marriage? And that your, er ... shall we say ... unusual lifestyle was the cause of a rift between you and your father?"

Nathan intervened. "With respect, could you please make sure your questions are pertinent to our investigation." He sounded annoyed, the professionalism no longer evident.

Once their attention had been deflected from enquiries about my private life and further attempts to elicit additional personal information were thwarted, they must have realised that this particular area of discussion had been closed off and the assembled members of the Press once again turned their attention to the investigation itself, addressing their questions to Nathan.

I barely heard it. All I could think of was the coming storm and the total destruction of my public reputation.

CHAPTER EIGHTEEN

Nathan stood with his back to me. Not speaking. He stared out through the rain-splattered window into the compound beyond, legs apart, hands behind his back, fists clenched.

Never one to readily show his emotions, he rarely gave himself away. But I had known him for a long time and even after all these years, I could still read the telltale signs that betrayed his darker moods; the silences, the turning away, the rigid stance.

And all the signs were there. He was angry. I didn't need to guess who with.

We were in Lowe's office. It had seemed as good a place as any to keep out of the way of the Press.

I was slumped down in a chair by Lowe's desk, still worrying about the unwarranted exposure of my personal life and trying not to think of the consequences.

In the corridor outside, people passed by as the press conference broke up. The hum of conversation and occasional burst of laughter contrasted sharply with the uncomfortable silence in the room. Nathan was not in a speaking mood but I needed to break the spell.

I said, "Are you angry with me or them?"

He grunted without turning. That answered my question. Just as I thought.

I snapped at him. "What do you have to be so angry about? I'm the one who took a hammering in there. Not you."

My carefully nurtured public reputation had been shattered, the broken remains of my private life exposed to anyone who wanted to pick over the pieces. He was the one who had subjected me to this. And yet I was the one being made to feel as if I had done something wrong.

"I'll tell you why," he said, turning to face me. "I'm angry because this sort of crap takes the focus away from the investigation. And that's what this press conference was for. Not to air your questionable personal habits in public."

"You think I wanted this?"

He snorted. "Well, no self-respecting person would that's for sure. You I'm not so sure about." He turned away and stood with his back to me again.

My face flushed. That stung. It shouldn't have mattered what he thought but it did. For once, I had nothing to say. No riposte. And so we lapsed into silence again.

Lowe had been helping to usher the press out of the station and eventually returned to let us know that the coast was clear. If he was aware of the strained atmosphere in the room, he didn't let it show.

"There are still one or two reporters hanging around," he said, "but most of them have moved on."

Nathan acknowledged this and said, "See if you can find a driver to take Mr MacGregor home."

He couldn't wait to get me out of there.

I opened my mouth to speak, hesitated, and then said, "I don't want to impose on you any more than necessary but would you mind if I hung on here a bit longer. Most of the press are staying at the Fairview. They'll be in the bar at this time of day and I'm not up to facing them yet."

I resented having to ask but the Fairview was the last place I wanted to be right then.

Nathan growled and muttered something under his breath.

It was hard to read his expression. I couldn't tell if it was one of pity or contempt.

"Wait here," he said and strode from the room. Lowe followed him, looking embarrassed, and closed the door behind him.

I rose from my chair, crossed over to the window, and stared out into the fading light. The day was as grey and miserable as my mood. Everyone seemed to be taking shots at me over the last few days. It was wearing me down and, right now, another barrage from the press was the last thing I needed.

Some minutes later, Nathan returned. "I called a friend of mine who has a holiday home in Fleming Road off the Esplanade," he said. "He's given his permission for you to stay there till the heat's off. The press aren't going to leave you alone any time soon so I suggest you take advantage of the offer. Okay?"

I accepted. It seemed the sensible thing to do. "That's very generous of him. Thank you."

"I don't want your thanks. It's my duty to protect you from this sort of unwarranted attention. Get your things and let's go."

God forbid he should appear to be doing me any favours.

"And keep your head down as we leave the yard," he said. "We don't want to be followed." He was already making his way out of the door.

I grabbed my coat from the back of the chair and hurried after him. He led the way through to the courtyard and we were soon on the road, heading towards the Esplanade in Nathan's Astra, having made it out of the compound without being spotted.

On the way, I made one or two feeble attempts at conversation, trying to ease the tension. Nathan wasn't buying it. Every time I opened my mouth, I provoked a grunt in response. The only sound inside the car was the relentless scrape of the wipers across the windscreen. And it grated on my nerves.

A few minutes of this and I'd had enough. I was worn out, miserable and fed up, and I'd be damned if I was going to take any more.

"For God's sake, Nathan. Ever since I got back you've given me the cold treatment. Either drop the attitude or talk to me about it."

Bad move.

He slammed on the brakes. Hard.

We slewed to a halt, skidding into the kerb. Tyres squealed beneath us. Burning rubber. I was thrown forward in my seatbelt, and then hurled back against the headrest.

The suddenness of his reaction shocked me.

Shaken, I reached out to steady myself against the dashboard and turned to face him.

He stared out through the windscreen into the murky light, his breathing slow and laboured as though he was struggling to control himself.

Perhaps that outburst hadn't been such a good idea after all. I'd provoked him into an even angrier mood.

I waited with trepidation to see what his next move would be.

He switched off the ignition.

Without turning, and in a voice that betrayed his barely controlled anger, he said, "I won't pretend I wasn't hurt when you walked out on me. And okay, I knew you had problems with your family. But we'd spent more than half our lives together and you walked away without a word or a backward glance. And I never heard from you again. How do you think that was for me?"

"Nathan ..."

"Shut up."

I shut up.

He continued, "Well, you know what, Mikey, I came to terms with what happened. We were still young men finding our way in life and I thought maybe my lifestyle wasn't for you. That you'd chosen another path in life. When I heard you'd married, that seemed to clinch it. So I let it go, thinking you'd made an honest choice and you'd moved on. Well, how wrong I was."

He turned to face me. His eyes blazed, and when he spoke again, there was a bitter edge to his voice. "You want to know why I'm so angry? It's because this is what you gave up our relationship for. This sordid pathetic excuse for a life. Is this all you ended up with, Mikey? Is this what you left me for? Is it?"

I blinked and turned away, unable to meet his gaze. My heart pounded. This was the emotional reckoning I had anticipated when we met two days ago. And now that it had finally erupted like this, I didn't know how to deal with it.

"Nothing to say?" He turned on the ignition. "Well, there's a surprise."

He didn't wait for an answer - not that I had one - just put the car into gear and drove off again.

CHAPTER NINETEEN

But for the constant rasp of the wipers and the clatter of rain on the roof, the rest of the journey passed in silence.

I huddled up against the side window, my shoulder pressed against the cold glass, still reeling from that unexpected broadside.

The worst of it was knowing he was right. I'd made a mess of my life. But I needed to make him understand how and why, and that we don't always get to choose our own paths through life, that there are so many pressures to conform, and sometimes we're left floundering, trying to make the best of the choices that are forced on us.

I shot him an occasional glance. He kept his eyes firmly fixed on the road ahead, jaw clenched, his knuckles white against the wheel. Until he had calmed down, there seemed little point in trying to explain. And so I kept quiet, enduring the uneasy silence, and when we reached our destination, it was a relief to get out of the car.

Nathan, still not speaking, led the way to the house, part of a row of old worker-style cottages in a cul-de-sac off the main road. He unlocked the door, pushed it open, and stood aside to let me in.

"You have a key." I said as I passed him.

"Yes." His tone was curt.

"A close friend?"

"None of your fucking business." He followed me in and closed the door behind him.

He was still seething, so I didn't bother to respond. Anything I said would only exacerbate his mood.

Until now I hadn't given much thought to Nathan's personal life. I'd been so wrapped up in my own problems, I'd not stopped to consider that he may have a relationship. Or relationships. But of course he would.

Nathan said, "I'll go back to the Fairview and ask Karen to pack your belongings. I'll be back with them as soon as possible.

In the meantime, stay out of sight. The press will be looking for you."

As he turned towards the door, he added, "Not that it should be a problem for you. You've become quite the expert at hiding."

So much for our amicable working relationship. As relationships went, it was anything but amicable and it certainly wasn't working. At least not for me.

"Did you ever ask yourself why," I said, "or is that all I get? Just a cheap shot?"

His hand on the door handle, he turned back to face me, nostrils flaring.

He was still angry. But what the hell. So was I. It was time to stand up for myself. I was tired of taking the blame for the choices I'd been forced to make.

I stepped towards him. "Well, guess what. The world doesn't revolve around you and your troubles. You think you were the only one who had a rough deal? Did you ever stop to think what I was going through while you were wallowing in your own self-pity?"

He let go of the handle and, with an angry growl, launched himself at me across the room, his face distorted with rage. "You fucking dare give me that crap after what you put me through?"

He grabbed me by the collar, slammed me against the wall.

The blunt force hit me hard. A shock of pain raced through my back and I cried out. Fear stirred inside me and pumped through my veins. So much anger.

"You fucking selfish shit." He was out of control.

I gasped for air. "I'm trying to make you understand." I shouted the words into his face. My chest tightened.

"Oh, I understand." He clutched the neck of my shirt in his fist and twisted it, his face close to mine. "You're spineless. Too much of a coward to face up to your problems. It was so much easier to run away, wasn't it, Mikey?" He spat the words at me, his body pressed against mine.

"That's not how it was." Adrenalin surged through me. I thrust an arm against his throat, forced him back.

He responded fast, grabbed my arm, twisted it to one side, pinned it against the wall. His chest heaved against mine, our faces almost touching. "That's just how it was. Time you manned up, Mikey, and took a good hard look at yourself. Time you took responsibility." With each jibe, he rammed me hard against the wall.

I gulped in more air, my free hand against his chest, trying to hold him back.

We both paused, gasping, and I steadied myself against him, his hard muscular thigh pressed against mine, his chest moving against me, his ragged breath on my cheek.

And at that moment, the unthinkable happened. A stirring in my loins.

In the heat of a fight, our primitive limbic brains, following their own primal instincts, wrest control from our conscious minds and flood our bodies with a mix of chemicals to boost our strength and stamina. They give us the energy we need to flee or stand our ground and fight. But it is this self same mix, adrenaline and neurotransmitters, that rouse us to satisfy our carnal needs.

It is well known amongst those for whom combat is a way of life that sexual arousal is all too often a consequence of those heightened emotions that aid them during conflict. And my body was responding to my own emotional high fuelled by the chemical surge that raced through my blood, seeking release.

At such times, our bodies don't listen to reason. Nor take account of our wider circumstances. And so, when I tried to quell the unbidden urge and push it from my mind, my body wouldn't let me. It was remembering. Recalling times past. It remembered the crush of his body against mine, the taste of his breath in my mouth, the strength in his arms, his smell.

I couldn't let this happen.

Writhing beneath his grasp, I fought for release and tried to push him away. But he was stronger and held me fast. I couldn't break free. Screwing my eyes tight shut, I tried to will my body into submission and bring it back under control. But in vain.

I hardened against him.

His response was immediate. With the shock of realisation, his hand tightened on my collar and his body stiffened. When I opened my eyes, he was staring directly into my face. The wide-eyed expression of surprise faded and he loosened his grip. A flicker of amusement crossed his face and his mouth curled. All I could do was stare back, at a loss to explain or rationalise what was happening.

Leaning even closer, he whispered, "Is this what you want Mikey? Is this how it is for you now?"

As he spoke, he pressed me to the wall and moved against me in that old familiar way, stirring up memory and desire and heat.

And in a single moment all the years fell away.

I wanted to stop him but I couldn't. My body responded to his, picking up familiar cues and matching his rhythm with my own. He played my body as he had so often before, moving me in ways I remembered well.

"Please, Nathan, please." I gasped for air, breathed in his musky scent.

His lips brushed my cheek and he murmured, "Please, 'yes' or please, 'no'." His breath was warm against my skin.

"I don't know," I said. But I knew. And when his lips sought mine, I pressed my mouth hard against his as the fire stirred in my loins. I arched my back, pressing into him, wanting him, all recent memory of anger and recrimination lost in the moment.

And for that one moment nothing else mattered but this overpowering need.

And then it was gone.

He pulled away and stood back, a look of undisguised contempt on his face. His mouth twisted into a sneer. "What a joke you are."

I cried out, confused and hurt, and slid down the wall onto the floor at his feet, shaken and sobbing. "Why?" I mewled.

But he didn't reply. He was already heading back towards the door.

"Please don't hate me."

He reached the door, turned back, and said, "I don't hate you.

I may have come close once. But not any more. Now I just pity you. You're just a sad sorry joke."

As he left, he added, "I'll send one of my men round with your belongings." And he was gone, slamming the door behind him.

I stayed down on the floor for what seemed like an age but was probably no more than a few minutes.

The look on his face in those final moments was burned into my mind. How he must have despised me. Had I done that to him? Made him so bitter? Had I been so focused on my own problems, I couldn't see the harm I was doing? Well I sure as hell knew now.

Bundled into a ball, I sat with my arms locked around my legs, rocking back and forth, my mind a roiling mix of confusion and despair. Eventually, I rolled over onto my knees and pushed myself to my feet. I was still shaking but my heart had stopped racing.

There was a set of yellow plastic chairs over by a matching plastic-topped kitchen table and I made my way over to one of them and dropped into it. The ground floor of the house was open plan, the furniture bland and utilitarian like the table I sat at. There were no personal items around, no ornaments. It was stark and empty. Like me. Like my life.

I didn't know what I was doing anymore, where I was going. My life was in meltdown. Two failed marriages, a father who had never liked me and an ex-lover who hated me.

One thing was for sure. I couldn't go on like this. Nathan was right; my life was a joke. What had I got to show for it? An expensive house in Mayfair; a flat in Islington; a car beyond the economic grasp of most people; the resources to enjoy the best of everything; a high profile public image, the clean-cut, well-connected man of means.

And here I was, on my own, incapable of sustaining a committed and loving relationship, snatching what intimate pleasures I could in back-street dives with anonymous strangers.

Well, no more. The experiences of the last few days had been a wake up call. It was time to face up to those past mistakes.

I took out my mobile and, with a shaking hand, tapped in the familiar number. Karen answered.

"Nathan is on his way to you. He's arranging to have my belongings picked up. Tell him not to bother. I'm on my way back."

CHAPTER TWENTY

It's amazing what a change of lighting can do for a place. The Fairview had been transformed.

Harsh overhead lighting had given way to the subdued amber glow of the wall lights spaced around the open reception area. Soft music played in the background, further improving the ambiance.

The low hum of voices and clink of glasses drifted out from the bar. Obviously, the hacks were making the most of their expense accounts.

By the reception desk, Nathan was in animated conversation with Karen. Judging by his expression, I guessed he had learned of my decision to return.

Karen was the first to see me approach. Her face creased into a show of concern.

Nathan followed her gaze and scowled when he saw me.

As I drew near, he reached out and grabbed me by the arm. In a low voice - presumably, so as not to draw attention from the bar - he said, "What the hell are you playing at?"

"I'm taking your advice."

That seemed to confuse him. He let go of my arm. "What?" He furrowed his brow.

Karen crossed her arms and said, "Would one of you please tell me what's going on here?" She glared at each of us in turn.

"I'm tired of hiding," I said.

Now it was Karen's turn to be confused.

But the light of recognition dawned in Nathan's eyes. "What are you thinking of doing, Mikey?" It sounded more like an admonition than a question.

I answered with a question of my own. "Why don't you both join me in the bar?"

I didn't wait for an answer.

One of Karen's hired helps, a harassed-looking young woman in a bright red tabard, was carrying a tray of food through the archway opposite to the dining room beyond. I followed behind her and turned into the bar.

Two reporters I recognised from the press conference were being served at the counter and a group of five more were seated around a larger table over by the window. I was pleased to see that John Chesterton, the sleazeball, wasn't amongst them. Even so, this wasn't going to be an easy ride.

One of the two men at the counter spotted me. "Hey. The wanderer returns. We thought you'd done a runner."

That raised a few hearty laughs from the others. They must have found out I'd been staying at the Fairview.

"How could I possibly pass up on the pleasure of your company?" I took a seat at the bar and ordered a double scotch from the bartender.

"I'll get that," the wisecracker said, producing a wallet. He was a heavy set man with a florid complexion which didn't go well with his bottle-green jacket.

"Damn right you will. Fair exchange for the lowdown on my private life I would have thought."

"Sure," he said, suddenly more alert. He held out a hand, "the name's Brian Driscoll, Sunday Echo."

I shook his hand. "I don't suppose there's much point introducing myself. By now, you probably know me as well as I know myself."

"Well not quite," Driscoll said. "But your wife has been very helpful with the more recent details."

This time I joined in the laughter. "She always did have a big mouth."

The bartender handed me a glass and I took a large swig.

The group by the window were paying more attention now. They had their notebooks at the ready.

Nathan and Karen had taken up positions by the open entrance to the bar. Nathan was scowling again but Karen still looked concerned.

I took another large swig of scotch and said, "Well, go ahead. What do you want to know?"

"I'm sure you know the answer to that." He reached into a

pocket and produced a notebook of his own." He held it up. "Do you mind?"

"Not at all."

"So is it true? You split from your wife?"

"Yes, it's true. And before you ask, yes, it was another man."

"You want to tell us about him?"

"No. I don't to drag him into it. It was nothing serious anyway."

"You were in the habit of having casual sexual relationships?" Driscoll jotted down notes as he spoke.

"Let's say I've had my moments."

"How did she find out?"

"She had me followed. And got some very good photos for her money. Maybe she'll let you have them. Some of them might even be printable."

Driscoll stopped scribbling and looked up. "You're being surprisingly candid. You do know what effect this is going to have, don't you? That blue-eyed wonder boy image of yours is going to be ripped to shreds."

"To hell with it."

I could already see the image that would be plastered over the front pages of the gossip mags. No matter how hard you tried to avoid it, the media always managed to get a shot of you looking like a deranged serial killer with an insane grin or a hollow-eyed degenerate with sunken cheeks. Bless them. They sure did like their stereotypes. I wondered which type of shot they would choose for me.

Driscoll continued to stare into my face.

"I've had good cause to rethink my life choices since coming back here." I drained my glass.

"You want to explain that?"

I signalled the bartender and held up my empty glass. He took it from me and refilled it. "This is on you too," I said to Driscoll.

He nodded. "On my tab," he said to the bartender and turned his attention back to me.

"Let me tell you something about my childhood here," I said.

And so it all came out. The whole sorry saga of life in a family oppressed by the iron will of a father who demanded nothing short of Godly perfection in all things, a control freak who saw any deviation from biblical teachings as a mortal sin, worthy of eternal damnation in the fires of hell.

"I'm not saying he was a bad man," I explained, "just misguided. In some ways he was a kindly considerate man who cared deeply for the well-being of his parishioners. But that was his public face. In private, with his family, he was a different man, overbearing and strict."

Driscoll and the other hacks scribbled furiously. I related the events of the night my father found out I was gay and in a relationship with another man. I declined to name names.

"You can imagine the effect that had on him," I said. "It was like our own private Third World War."

I explained how, still a young man, still influenced by my parent's values, I had tried to be the respectful god-fearing son rather than live with my father's contempt.

"It mattered to me what they thought."

"And now?"

"And now? Enough is enough. I was stupid. I've been a fool and wasted my life living a lie. I thought it was more important to live up to someone else's ideal of the sort of life I should lead, instead of just being myself. And I've hurt too many people along the way, myself as much as anyone else."

"Where do you go from here?"

"I don't know. Coming back here stirred up old memories. Of a time when I still had my whole life in front of me and I still had choices to make."

I explained how, by making all the wrong choices, I had lost what chance of happiness I had with the one person who ever mattered.

"It's too late to change the past," I said, "but one thing I do know is that I won't live a lie any more. From now on, I'll live the life I want. If I'd been honest with myself and everyone else, none of this would have mattered."

"What about your show? Will you carry on with that?"

"I haven't made any decisions yet. Though it's possible that's one decision that will be made for me."

I couldn't imagine the BBC being too happy about renewing my contract after I'd tarnished my reputation in such a dramatic way. I put my empty glass on the bar and slid off the stool. "And now if you'll excuse me gentlemen. It's been a long day. And I need some down time."

I left them still scribbling away in the bar. Nathan was still standing in the doorway but he wasn't scowling anymore. Karen looked as worried as ever. I didn't acknowledge either of them. Time to get away. I stepped outside and held my face up to the rain as I crossed towards the Elan, enjoying the feel of it against my skin. It was fresh and clean.

CHAPTER TWENTY-ONE

It was raining hard by the time I reached the cliff top. I pulled over to the far side of the road where the ground dropped down into the valley below.

A thick blanket of dark cloud hovered over the town like a bad dream. Street lamps were already going on all over Elders Edge, flickering into lambent life in defiance of the growing darkness and turning the highways and byways into snaking lines of light.

I was wrecked, physically and emotionally drained. Another day like this I could do without. Between the relentless basting of the press and Nathan's emotional battering, it was like being tossed around by a force ten gale. My head was all over the place. I leaned back against the headrest and tried to relax. The press confrontation had been daunting. And the fallout from that was a joy to look forward to.

Then there had been Nathan's furious outburst. Bad enough in itself. But the worst of it, what disturbed me the most, had been my own reaction. I had been aroused, excited. Those feelings had come out of nowhere and had shaken me. And as much as I tried, I couldn't understand. Why now, after all this time? Had those feelings always been there, suppressed? It didn't make any sense. I closed my eyes and tried to clear my mind.

The beating of the rain on the roof of the Elan had a soothing soporific effect, and as the minutes passed, I drifted into a light doze.

Through the sound of the driving rain, I didn't hear the other car approach. It was only when I heard the door slam shut, startling me back into full awareness, that I became conscious of it and opened my eyes to see who was there. Nathan was heading towards me, hurrying through the rain.

A knot tightened in my stomach. I recalled all those times he'd known to find me here when I was troubled, and come to my aid. But why was he here now? It was difficult to believe my emotional welfare was one of his prime concerns. Especially after that last traumatic skirmish. I hoped this wasn't going to be another angry confrontation.

For the briefest of moments, I considered locking the door and leaving him standing in the rain. I was still hurt and confused and embarrassed. And I wasn't in the mood for company. Especially not his. But good grace won out over rancour and, reluctantly, I leaned over and opened the passenger side door.

He slid in next to me.

"You're the last person I expected to see," I said.

He closed the door. "I knew you'd be here. Where else would you go at a time like this?"

"Some things never change do they?"

We sat in silence. The rain hammered out its staccato rhythm on the roof. I waited for him to say what was on his mind, whatever it was that had brought him here.

Eventually, he said, "What you just did. It was either very brave or very foolish."

"Probably both."

Silence again.

"Did you mean everything you said back there?"

"About being stupid? Oh, yes. I meant every word of it."

"About making the wrong choices."

"That too." What was he driving at here? Was he looking for an explanation?

I searched his face for some indication of his mood. But he was expressionless, staring out through the windscreen. He was holding his emotions in check, as he so often did, keeping them hidden beneath that impenetrable facade. Which is why his recent outburst had been such a shock. So unlike him. He must have been hurting.

I said, "I know how selfish I was, leaving the way I did. I know what a jerk I was."

"Mikey ..."

"Let me finish." I continued, "If I have any defence at all, it's that I was going through an emotional hell. After my father found out about us ... well, you knew what he was like. It was a bad time and I wasn't thinking straight. But did you really think I didn't care?"

"I didn't know what to think. I just knew you were gone."

Was it worth raking over the ashes, stirring up a past that was dead and buried? Maybe it was. I owed him something. "I loved you. And once I'd made the decision to leave - rightly or wrongly - I knew I couldn't face you and still go through with it."

My throat was dry. I swallowed and said, "My heart was breaking. But I thought I was doing the right thing, the proper thing. I wish now that I'd found the courage to stand up to my father. But I didn't. And I paid a high price for it. I lost you."

"I wish I'd been there to stop you."

"So do I."

"I'd always thought that I wasn't enough. That what we had wasn't enough."

"Did you think it would be easy breaking free of all those years of conditioning? It's easy now to see how wrong I was. But not back then. When it mattered."

"You never thought to get in touch?"

"Yes, of course I did. Not at first. I was trying to forget you. Later, when I realised what a mistake I'd made. But, by then, it was too late. Too much time had gone by. And so I let it go. I never did forget you though. However hard I tried. But I had to move on and make a life for myself."

"Mikey ...". He faltered, as if searching for the right words. "What happened earlier. All that ... I had no right to treat you like that. It was unforgivable. I'm sorry."

Is this why he was here? To make the peace? I hoped so.

I snorted. "I'm sure I deserved it."

"No, you didn't. That wasn't about you. It was me. I was angry. Seeing you again after all these years brought it all back. All that resentment. And then when I heard about the breakup of your marriage. The reason for it. It all boiled over. But I had no right to take it out on you."

"I guess you had good cause." I had some explaining to do too. "What happened back there. I mean at the end." Finding the right words was hard. "I didn't mean that to happen. I don't know why it did."

A pause. And he said, "I understand."

I'm not sure he did. But then neither did I.

We sat and watched the rain.

There was so much more I wanted to say. But I didn't know how. Once, all those years ago, there was nothing I couldn't have told him. Back then, it would have been hard to believe we could drift so far apart. How easy it was to take for granted those relationships most precious to us. And how easy to recognise their value only when we've lost them. But maybe there was a way to come to terms with what had happened and repair some of the damage done. And maybe he could find a way to forgive me. I hoped so.

I leaned against the steering wheel, laughed and pointed down into the half-darkness. "Do you remember that time I whitewashed the greengrocer's window? The shop's still over there."

"I remember it was my dad who caught you."

"I didn't think anyone would be around at that time in the morning."

"My dad was always out early on his beat."

"I liked your dad. He always treated me like one of the family."

Nathan grunted. "He was far too easy on you. If his sergeant had caught you, it would have been a different matter. You used to get into so many mindless scrapes."

"I see the Post Office has gone."

"Yes, I wasn't sorry to see it go."

We both knew why. I didn't need to ask. It was where Nathan's father had lost his life. He'd died of a gunshot wound following an abortive raid on the Post Office. It had been one of those momentous events that had rocked the sleepy town to its core and had made a hero of Jonathan Quarryman. I'm sure it was then that Nathan had decided to follow in his father's footsteps, to honour his memory.

"If your dad had still been around, do you think he would have minded? About us?"

He was quiet for a moment. I guessed he was thinking it over. He said, "I'd like to think he would have been okay with it. He might not have understood but one thing he always taught me was to stand up for myself, do what I thought was right. I'd like to think he would have respected any choices I made."

"Unlike my father."

Nathan grunted again.

"Sometimes," I said, "over the years, if ever I had a problem to sort out or a difficult decision to make, I would try to imagine what your advice would be. You were always the one I turned to for help. You kept me grounded. So, in my mind, I would ask your advice."

"And did I give you good advice?"

"Yes," I said. "But I didn't always take it." I grinned

"Nothing new there then." He turned to me and smiled.

"No." It was good to see that smile again.

The rain was heavier now. It clattered on the roof. The town below was a blur on the windscreen.

"So what now? What will you do?" he asked

"I'll have to learn to live with the consequences of my mistakes. And try not to make any more."

He grunted again. And then, "Are you happy, Mikey?"

A lump came to my throat. "Not yet," I whispered. "But I'm going to try."

The pounding rhythm of rain on the roof slowed as the sudden squall passed and the heavy downpour eased to a lighter rain. The town came back into focus on the windscreen.

"How about you?" I asked. "Anyone in your life?"

"No one special. I guess I've been alone too long to settle down now. I'm not sure I'd be any good in a relationship."

"Yes, you would. I can vouch for that. Any time you need a reference, just let me know." I shot him a smile.

"I'll bear it in mind."

We listened to the rain some more.

I said, "Right now, I need to stick around until this sorry mess is sorted. And I'll have to take care of my father's estate. There'll be a lot of paperwork to sort out. I should be here for a while yet."

"I got word back from Lowe earlier. Forensics have finished their work at the vicarage. You're free to go back there now."

"Thanks. And while I'm here, would you mind if I stayed on at your friend's place? Would he be okay with that? It'll be quieter there now the press have taken over the Fairview."

"Sure. It'll be fine. In fact, come on." He opened the door and pulled up his collar ready to brave the run back to his own car. "Let's go pick up your stuff and I'll help you settle in."

It seemed we'd come to a truce of sorts. It was never going to be the same between us. Not after everything that had happened. But maybe we could try to get along. Be friends again. At least, it was a start.

CHAPTER TWENTY-TWO

"What a pleasant smell." I wrinkled my nose against the stench. "That subtle aromatic blend of rotting garbage and cat piss. They go so well together."

I stepped around a pile of unrecognisable unsavoury-looking detritus and negotiated the rest of the narrow alley, taking care not to come into contact with the wet slime-stained walls.

"That's gross," said Nathan. "Is that what it is?" He followed behind me.

"Either that or you need to change your aftershave."

"Careful. Any more cracks like that and you'll find yourself sitting in one of those trashcans."

There was laughter in his voice so I knew I didn't need to take him too seriously.

I wasn't usually in the habit of sneaking around alleyways at night but there was no other way to reach the back door of the Fairview's domestic quarters without being spotted from the public area. The media guys were still in the bar - the general hum of their chatter filtered through the brightly-lit window that looked out on the alley at its far end - and I didn't want to risk running into any of them. I'd bared my soul enough for one lifetime. To be extra cautious, we'd dropped my car back at the house and driven over in Nathan's Astra. A bright-yellow Elan might be a bit of a giveaway. Nathan thought I was being overly-paranoid but he was prepared to indulge me for once.

The back door was locked but Karen had given me a set of keys that included the ones to her private entrance. It saved having to go through the public areas which was just as well in the circumstances.

The young girl who had served the guests earlier was taking a break in the back office. Her name was Jenny. Karen was busy serving in the bar so I left a message to let her know I would call later and we climbed the back stairs to my room.

Nathan seemed more like his old self. Not exactly talkative. That had never been his way. He was more the speak-when-you-have-something-to-say type. But he seemed more relaxed. And he'd stopped treating me like a stranger. I was still wary though. That angry battering had left its mark.

I dragged my two suitcases from under the bed and Nathan emptied the wardrobe. I asked him how the investigation was going. "The reason for Black's absence could be genuine," I said. "So are you looking for anyone else?"

Nathan dropped my clothes onto the bed. "Until we have something more positive, anyone and everyone is a suspect."

"Including me?" I emptied the chest of drawers and threw the rest of my clothes on top of the others.

Nathan turned away from the wardrobe, holding a pair of shoes, and glowered at me. "Come on, Mikey. We wouldn't even be having this conversation if I thought that. You know we have to go through the motions."

"I guess so."

Nathan grunted. "God knows you've caused me some grief over the years. But I know you better than that." He dropped the shoes into a suitcase.

"I'd like to think so."

I finished folding and packing the clothes and we carried the cases out to the Astra. I held the cases while Nathan unlocked and opened the boot, and I dropped them in.

"I hear what you say about Black," Nathan said, "but some things don't add up. The message he left at the surgery for instance."

"I wondered about that too."

We made our way around to the front of the car and Nathan went on to explain. "Why leave a text message when he could so easily have phoned? All I can come up with is that, for some reason, he hadn't wanted to be overheard."

The practice manager at the surgery had thought the same. I had my own theory but I kept it to myself for the moment.

Nathan climbed into the driver's seat and I slid into the passenger seat beside him.

He said, "We have to think about opportunity too. Apart from the vicarage and the curate's residence, Black's house is the only other one at that end of Vicarage Lane."

He started the car and we drove off in the direction of Fleming Road. "Unless someone came by foot through the woods at the other side of the cul-de-sac, anyone but Black would have to approach from the High Street at the other end of the road."

"Yes, of course," I said. And then a sudden brainwave. "Is there any CCTV in the area?"

"Already onto it. The bank at the end of the High Street has good coverage. We might get something useful there. Lowe and his team are already looking through the footage."

"Of course, someone might have come through the woods. There'd be no chance of getting anything useful then."

"Sure but that's only likely if your father's murder had been planned. And only if our man had thought about the possibility of surveillance. It could have been a spur of the moment attack for all we know. We have to cover all possibilities."

We reached the house and Nathan pulled in to the kerb. "In the meantime," he said, "we have enough to justify a warrant to search Black's place, so that's our next move. We'll get a warrant sworn out tomorrow."

Nathan fetched the cases from the boot and I unlocked the door to let us in.

Maybe now would be a good time to press him again about my taking a more active part in the investigation. I didn't want to push my luck but it was worth a try. "I know you said you didn't want any outside interference but I would like some input. And I do have some expertise; witness interviews, crime scene investigation, that sort of thing. I could help."

He didn't respond immediately. Once inside, he dropped my luggage on the floor and said, "Okay. You're on the team. But only so I can keep an eye on you." He raised a warning finger. "But I don't want you going off at a tangent on your own. Nothing unauthorised. Understood?"

I gritted my teeth. "Understood."

"I mean it, Mikey. You leave this to the police. You hear me?"

"You got it."

"I'll leave you to unpack then." At the door, he turned back. "You need any help sorting out your father's stuff?"

"Thanks but I have it covered. Karen's coming over with me in the morning."

"Okay. I'll catch up with you later then. We'll have the search warrant for Black's place in the morning so I'll pick you up from the vicarage on the way. And don't forget what I told you."

"I hear you."

I stood in the doorway as he made his way to the car. He'd started to bully me around again. As he always had in the past. A warm glow spread through me. It was good to have the old Nathan back.

CHAPTER TWENTY-THREE

I chilled out for the rest of that evening. After the events of the last few days, I needed some time to relax. I poured myself a very large glass of a fine Cabernet Sauvignon I'd brought back from the Fairview and slipped a copy of Tchaikovsky's First Piano Concerto into the disk player. I'd found the disk in Barwell's CD rack. It was good to know Nathan had friends with taste. I settled myself into an easy-chair and let the wine and the music work their magic on my frayed nerves.

The London Symphony Orchestra was onto the second movement when the phone rang. And rang. And rang. It was my agent, Jerry Martin. It meant only one thing; the evening papers were out on the shelves. After four missed calls, I answered it. He was persistent, I'll give him that.

"Hi, Jerry."

"What the fuck have you done?"

"Yes, I'm fine, Jerry. Thanks for asking."

"Cut the sarcasm, Mikey. I'm not in the mood. What the fuck were you thinking. Have you seen the papers?"

"No, not yet. Anything interesting?"

"It's a disaster."

"Don't tell me Man City have lost to Spurs?"

"You know damn well what I'm talking about. Listen to this." The rustle of a newspaper. "I've been a fool."

"Jerry, don't be so hard on yourself."

"Not me. You. Your words. That's the headline."

I was contrite. It was part of Jerry's job to manage my public image and I'd put him in an awkward position. I shouldn't wind him up like this.

"I'm sorry, Jerry. It was all going to come out anyway. The best I could do was try to manage it. But it was never going to do my image much good whichever way I played it."

There was a long audible sigh from the other end of the phone. "Look, I don't give a damn what you do in your private life. I really don't. But unfortunately, the douche bags of the Press do. So I'll tell you how we'll play this. The public always like someone who faces up to their faults. The bad boy looking for redemption. It's a Brit thing. So we'll go with that. Really push it home. And for the moment, I'll hold fire on renegotiating your contract with the BBC. Wait till the dust has settled. Okay?"

"Okay." There was a lump in my throat. "Seriously, Jerry, I do appreciate everything you do for me. You know that."

"Yeah, well you sure do make me earn my fees. Just leave it to me. And look after yourself, you hear? And try to stay out of more trouble. Ciao."

The phone clicked. And rang again. It was a colleague in London. I turned off my mobile. I wasn't in the mood for more calls. Or anything else for that matter.

After Jerry's call, I found it difficult to relax again. I was restless.

Nathan had given the all clear for access to my father's vicarage and right then seemed as good a time as any to go over there, take a look around and maybe make a start on sorting through his papers. On the way, I could drop by the Fairview and let Karen know I had moved out.

The rain was holding off, so I walked over, taking the long route around to the rear of the building, and let myself in through the back door.

Karen was in her private sitting room. She'd been reading through the evening paper when I interrupted her.

"Any of our wonderful boys from the Fourth Estate still around?" I asked.

"In the bar as usual." She held the paper out to me, holding it between thumb and forefinger as if it was contaminated. "Have you seen this?"

"I've heard about it. My agent called. You can hold back on the details for the moment. I'm not in the mood."

"Probably for the best," she said, dropping it onto the couch, a look of disgust on her face.

I said, "I called in to let you know I've moved my stuff out. Nathan found me a bolt hole to hide away in."

"Yes, he told me. Brandon Barwell's place."

"You know him?"

"He was a regular guest here till he bought his own place. And I've seen him and Nathan around together since then."

My heart jumped. "Are they an item?"

Karen held out a hand, rocked it from side to side. "It's an on-off sort of thing as far as I know. Nothing serious."

I was relieved. Not that I had any right to be. It wasn't my concern after all. "Well, I'm grateful to him whatever he is. He's done me a favour."

"I'll drive over and pick you up in the morning on the way to the vicarage. Probably best if we take my car."

I agreed. "I'm on my way over there now. Might as well take a look around and see what needs doing."

As I was leaving, I said, "No Sgt Lowe tonight?"

"He's on duty again." She sounded peeved.

"Oh well, the course of true love never did run smooth."

The screwed-up newspaper hit me in the back as I left.

CHAPTER TWENTY-FOUR

My father's study seemed so much smaller than I remembered it. The room was windowless and airless, and the walls and furnishings already bore the stale musty odour of neglect.

A large mahogany desk dominated the room. I sat in the swivel chair behind it, trying it out for size, and switched on the metal cantilever lamp at its side.

I hated this room. Always had. It had been the scene of too many unpleasant confrontations. My father would be seated behind this desk, face florid with anger, and rail at me for my many failings, and I would stand before him, head bowed, but defiant, and dream of the day I could get away from his oppressive control.

The room had seemed larger then, intimidating. But now it was just another room, shrunk back to normal size.

The desk drawers were locked. I tried each of the keys Trivett had given me until I found the one that fitted the central locking system, and opened all the drawers. The smaller drawers on the left contained various items of stationery; boxes of rubber bands, staples, a computer memory stick, and various bills, receipts and credit card statements. I emptied these into one of the plastic carriers bags I'd brought with me before turning my attention to the two larger drawers on the right. This is where my father kept his more important documents. I searched through them until I found the one I was looking for and put the others into another carrier, intending to look through them later. There was a large old-fashioned Remington typewriter on the desk and I pushed it to one side and spread the document out on the desk before me. It was my father's will.

When he had learned of my relationship with Nathan, one of my father's more immediate reactions was to threaten to disinherit me and I'd often wondered how serious he was. I opened up the document and read through it.

My spirits sank. True to his word, he had made no provision for me. Giles Trivett and a local solicitor were to be appointed his executors, and what assets he had were to be sold and the proceeds to be divided amongst a number of charities. There was no mention of me.

I sat back in the chair and let it sink in. I was saddened. It wasn't the thought of not benefiting financially - God knows, I had ample enough means of my own - but that he had still chosen to judge me so harshly, even after all these years, even after trying for so long to please him, to conform to his perception of the son he'd wanted me to be. All for nothing.

After dropping the document into the second bag with the other papers, I carried both bags into the hall, left them by the outer door, and toured the house.

Worn floorboards creaked and groaned underfoot as I passed over them. The old grandfather clock in the hall ticked patiently, and the complaining wind howled and rattled the windows and doors.

I wandered aimlessly through the rooms, reliving the past, each room conjuring up images and events from my youth. There were no happy memories here.

In the living room, I stared down at the chair where the body had been found. My father's favourite armchair. He would sit here in the evenings, at the end of his working day and either read or listen to the radio. This too is where my mother would keep him company, seated in the matching armchair on the other side of the fireplace. Sometimes, it would be one of his parishioners. Someone in need of advice or help.

Is that what had happened here that day? Had someone been seated in this other chair, in conversation with my father? What was it that had so roused them to anger they were moved to kill him in such a brutal way?

I stood there for a while, staring long and hard, as if the very act would conjure up an image of the events that had led to his death.

I shuddered and left the room, grabbed the bags from beside the door, and left the house, eager to be free of both it and the memories it stirred up.

The skies were clear. A full moon shone down, bleaching the surrounding landscape with its silvery glow. Across the road, beyond the ashen trees and behind a low stone wall, Black's house loomed out of the half-light like a squat grey beast.

On a whim, after dropping my bags into the boot of the Elan, I fished a flashlight out of the toolbox, and made my way over there, crunching half-frozen puddles underfoot. It couldn't do any harm to have a quick look around, see if I could spot anything unusual. And despite what Nathan might think, I wasn't exactly interfering. It's not like I was interviewing witnesses or anything. Just observing.

I circled the house and checked the door and windows for any signs of forced entry. Nothing. Next, I checked the garage. The door was secure but there was a side window. Inside the garage was a Ford Mondeo.

I scanned the surrounding area. There was a small iron gate behind the house which opened into the woods beyond. It would be an ideal access point for anyone wishing to avoid being seen on the road.

Again, I circled the house, this time shining my torch through each of the lower windows in turn. I was struck by how precisely everything was arranged in each room. In the kitchen, a magnetic wall rack held a set of knives, evenly and accurately spaced, carefully aligned and placed in order of length. A set of saucepans were laid out in a perfect line, all their handles pointing out at the same angle. So too, in the study. A laptop computer sat square and centred on the desk, a row of pens on one side of it and a paper knife and stapler on the other, all precisely aligned. It was the same in all the rooms; ornaments and furnishings carefully arranged and ordered.

The exception was the living room. A used coffee mug sat on a side table by the settee. The pages of a newspaper lay strewn around the floor with a crumpled cushion nearby. In any other setting, such minor disorder would have seemed normal. But in a house where neatness was carried to such an extreme, it seemed out of place, as if Black had left in a hurry and not had time to clear up after himself. If I'd been asked to assess Black's behaviour on what I'd seen here, I would be inclined to suspect him of having a compulsive obsessive disorder.

Satisfied that I had seen enough, I made my way back around the house. As I turned the corner to the front, I heard the clang of the gate. The unexpected sound startled me. I stopped and listened. The wind soughed through the trees and somewhere in the distance an owl hooted. All else was silent.

I turned back and, keeping the wall close to my right, crept around to the rear of the building, to within sight of the gate. It was open. I was sure it had been closed when I first saw it. I flashed the torch around the yard, checking out the deeper shadows and then turned the beam to the woods beyond the gate. Shadows danced and leapt around the trees as I moved the beam, making any possibility of seeing independent movement difficult. I turned off the torch and stood for a few moments until my eyes adjusted to the change of light and, by the glow of the moon, scanned the woods again.

Nothing seemed out of place. And yet I had the strangest sensation of being watched.

And something else. Right on the edge of awareness. A sound? I strained to hear. And there it was. A squelching. Slow and steady and repetitive. Like the sound of mud underfoot. Moving toward me.

A stray cloud crossed in front of the moon and the shadows around me shifted and deepened. I stepped back, seeking the darker shadows, and caught my elbow on the wall. My hand spasmed and the torch dropped from my grasp, clattering onto the stone flags. The sound reverberated around the courtyard, harsh and metallic, drowning out the natural night sounds.

The squelching stopped.

I held my breath.

Out in the darkness, someone or something was listening.

With a thudding heart and a hand pressed against the damp wall behind me, I slowly lowered myself to a crouch and felt around the ground. The stone flags were cold and clammy against my searching fingers. My hand brushed against something rough and hard. A large stone. I picked it up and groped around with my free hand. I found the torch, pocketed it, and rose to my feet. Taking a firm stand, I raised my hand high and hurled the stone towards the woods. It landed with a splatter on the far side of the wall.

Something squelched towards it.

That was my cue. I beat a hasty retreat, raced around the corner, and headed away from the house. Maybe I was being over-imaginative. Maybe I'd just interrupted some prowling night creature. But I wasn't going to stick around to find out. Clutching my coat collar, I leaned into the wind, head down, and hurried towards the road.

I looked up momentarily. Something moved. Ahead of me, a shape, darker than the rest, detached itself from the background and closed in. Straight towards me. I cried out, stopped and froze where I stood, muscles tensed. Fists clenched, I braced myself ready for action.

"What are you doing here?" It was Lowe.

"Jeez, man." I relaxed and dropped my fists. "I was about to thump you."

A short sharp laugh. "I wouldn't advise it. That way lies a whole heap of trouble."

"I was over at the vicarage. Thought I might take a look around as I was here."

"I saw your torch beam. What were you looking for?"

"Nothing in particular. Anything that seemed unusual."

"And of course, we've not thought of that. We needed you to do our job for us."

A well-deserved rebuke. "Sorry. I didn't mean to tread on any toes. I felt I should be doing something."

His tone lightened. "I know how frustrating it must be. But we're on top of it. We're keeping an eye on the place. I was on my usual patrol when I spotted you."

I gestured toward the far side of the courtyard. "Well you might want to check out the grounds behind the house. Maybe

I'm being paranoid but I thought I heard someone moving around and use the gate a few minutes ago."

"Let's go see."

I followed him across the courtyard, side-stepping the puddles.

Lowe swung the gate back and forth a few times. "It's heavy but it's also loose and the catch is rusted so it won't lock in place. Are you sure it wasn't just the wind? There are some strong gusts tonight."

"I guess it could be. Maybe I was spooked."

"I'll check the doors just in case."

"I've already done that. And the windows. They're all secure."

Lowe looked at me askance as if about to criticise me again for interfering. Instead he said, "I'll walk you back to the road. There's nothing more we can do here."

On the way, he said, "I know it must seem like nothing is happening but there's a lot going on behind the scenes."

"I know that. Nathan has been keeping me up to date." We reached the road and I said, "I hear you've been checking out some CCTV footage. Anything useful there?"

"We've identified most of the vehicles using Vicarage Lane over the past few days. Almost all of them are accounted for. We're still trying to trace a white Fiat Punto. We didn't get a registration but we're checking the DLVA records to see if anyone locally owns one."

"Good luck with that," I said.

It was after we'd parted company and I was walking back home that I remembered I'd seen a white Fiat Punto recently. I checked my watch. Too late to take it any further now but I would call in at the station in the morning to see Lowe and pass on what I knew. Maybe we were getting somewhere at last.

CHAPTER TWENTY-FIVE

I wrapped my hands around a mug of hot steaming coffee, enjoying its rich aroma. A warm glow spread through my fingers.

The following day had dawned colder than ever and I was slowly thawing out. It was still early morning and Lowe and I were sat at his desk in front of a monitor screen watching footage of traffic moving back and forth between the end of the High Street and Vicarage Lane. A fan heater on the wall above the desk warmed us. Karen had dropped me off on the way to the vicarage and I'd arranged to meet her there later.

"Jeez, is police work always this exciting?" I said.

Lowe sniffed. "Welcome to the real world. It's not all car chases and shootouts. In fact, it almost never is."

He sounded disappointed.

"How many of these have you had to sit through?" I said.

"Just two. There are ten all together, the last a couple of days ago, but my team have been sharing the task." He pointed at the screen. "This is the second one. It's when the Punto first appears."

We watched the screen and I sipped my coffee. The fan heater hummed in the background and the faint sound of a clattering keyboard filtered through from the room next door.

A grey Renault Megane appeared on the screen. "Who's that?" I said.

"Giles Trivett. He was on his way to a conference. The Fiat shows up about an hour later." He leaned over and hit the fast-forward button on the disk player. The Fiat appeared on the screen and he hit the play button. "There it is."

I leaned closer and peered at the image on the screen. "Yes, I have seen it before. That orange sticker in the back window. I remember it. It belongs to Adam Corby. He was working on it when I went to see Erin Corby."

"Corby. That rings a bell." Lowe reached across the desk and pulled a manila file towards him. He flipped it open and scanned through the pages. "Here it is. He and his wife are on the interview list. You know them?"

"I met them recently. Erin Corby was my father's cleaner."

He checked his file again. "Yes, I have a record of that. Could she have been on her way to the vicarage?"

"I doubt it. My father called her that week to put her off. He wasn't feeling too well." I drank some more of my coffee.

Lowe was still looking through the file. "We interviewed them both and have details of their movements over the last few days. There's no record of any visits to Vicarage Lane." He ran his finger down the page. "And the car shows up several times over the next few days."

"Erin cleaned for my father just once a week. So she wouldn't be visiting him anyway. At least not to work."

Lowe said, "You'd be surprised how often people miss out the more mundane details of their regular daily routines. It's a blind spot. They take them for granted and think them insignificant, not worth mentioning." He turned off the player. "It might be nothing but I'll follow it up this morning."

On the screen, the Corbys' car reappeared, on its way back to the High Street, passing a Transit Van going in the opposite direction. "Wait," I said and put a restraining hand on Lowe's arm. "Who's that?"

"That's Jonas Wainwright's van. He was on his way to visit your father. That was the day he heard your father arguing with his visitor."

I leaned back and folded my arms. "So all the vehicles are now accounted for?"

"Yes. All here." He tapped the manila folder in front of him. "I've been looking through the report compiled from my team's observations. And it makes for some very interesting reading."

"You got some useful info from it?"

"Very much so. There's not a lot of activity, Vicarage Lane being a cul-de-sac. Jonas' van shows up again a couple of days later as well as Trivett returning from his conference. Apart from a child's bike and some delivery vans, all of which have been accounted for and the drivers interviewed, that's it."

He closed the file and pushed it to one side. "But," he

continued, emphasising the word as if to point up the significance of what was to follow, "no sign of Black's Mondeo."

"His car is still in the garage. I saw it last night. Which begs the question of how Black left home. Is there any sign of him on foot?"

Lowe shook his head. "Which suggests to me one of two possibilities. Either Black left home in one of the vehicles recorded on the tapes. And, frankly, that doesn't strike me as likely. If he was leaving town, he would have driven himself or hired a taxi. Or he never left home at all."

He sank back into his chair.

I agreed with him. "Not unless he hiked through the woods, which would make no sense at all. And that means he must still be there. Somewhere."

As if on cue, we simultaneously turned to face each other. It was obvious from the look on his face that we were sharing the same thought.

"Are you thinking what I'm thinking?" I said.

Lowe grimaced. "We may have been heading in the wrong direction. Far from being the perpetrator of any crime, Black may well be another victim."

It was a reasonable assumption but there was another possibility. "You don't suppose he could be lying low at home?"

"Not unless he's lying low upstairs in total darkness. We've been keeping a close eye on the place."

We sat in silence for a few moments as the implications of our joint reasoning sank in.

I let out a long low whistle. "This could change everything. So what happens now?"

"Once the Chief has my report, he'll need to ratify my conclusions. But we'll have a better idea of the situation once we've searched Black's place. The Chief is on his way over from Charwell to give a briefing later this morning and then we're going over there this afternoon to carry out the search."

"Yes, he's arranged to pick me up from the vicarage on the way over. Which reminds me ..." I glanced at my watch. "In all the excitement of watching this fascinating stuff, I'd completely forgotten about Karen." I drained my mug, placed it on the desk and pushed myself to my feet. "I'd better get back over there and give her a hand."

"Karen's over at the vicarage?" Lowe stood up, reached over the desk, and switched off the player. "I'll give you a lift."

I winked at him. "All in the line of duty, eh?"

He flushed.

CHAPTER TWENTY-SIX

We made it to the vicarage to find Karen tight-lipped and short-tongued. Her way of letting me know she wasn't overjoyed at having been left alone for so long. But she soon brightened up when she saw Lowe's smiling face. And when he offered to take her out to dinner that evening, she begrudgingly forgave me.

Lowe went back to the station for his briefing leaving Karen and me to sort through my father's belongings.

Karen had already made a start. She'd bagged up some clothes and left them on the dining room table together with a heap of folded bedding too large to be bagged and various papers she had found lying around.

I'd brought back the bag of documents I'd found earlier, including the will - it made more sense to sort through them here - and I piled them on the table with the other documents and then took a tour of the house, checking through all the drawers and cupboards to make sure no papers had been missed. I added what I found to the pile on the dining table and then helped Karen sort through and bag up the rest of the clothing.

We were kept busy until well into the afternoon, dividing our time between work and heated discussions about the more dubious reasons for my newfound publicity.

We covered a range of fascinating subtopics. Such as why I was so bad at relationships and how someone who was supposed to be intelligent made so many stupid mistakes. One thing I could say about Karen is that she didn't pull her punches.

Whilst Karen was still in full flow about the many ways in which I chose to screw up my life, a police car passed the window on its way to Black's house, and a few minutes later, I was saved from any further debate by the timely arrival of Nathan's Astra.

He stayed long enough to pass the time of day with Karen and then we left her to it and trudged over to Black's place where a couple of constables were already standing by the door. Mr Dawson, the locksmith, was in attendance, drill at the ready.

"Okay, men, let's do it," said Nathan, and gave Dawson the go ahead.

Dawson acknowledged us with a nod and turned his attention to the door. He soon had it open. Nathan led the way into the house, followed by the two constables, and with me in the rear. Dawson hovered outside.

I paused and peered into each of the rooms as we passed by on our way through the house.

At the door into the living room, Nathan said, "Don't disturb anything." This was directed at me.

"I'm not an idiot."

He grunted and led the way into the room.

While I took stock of my surroundings, Nathan barked some orders and directed his men to various parts of the house to look around.

I waited until he had finished and said, "Any idea what you're looking for?"

"To be frank, I thought we might find a body."

"Looks like we might be thinking along the same lines. Lowe and I came to the same conclusion"

"Yes, I have his report. So let's hear your thoughts."

"A few things don't add up. His car for starters. It's still in the garage. If he was leaving town, why would he not use it?"

"Because it could be identified. But it's something to consider. Okay, next."

"There's no sign of Black or his car on the CCTV footage. All the other vehicles on the recordings are now accounted for and their drivers have been interviewed. They all seem to be in the clear so far. That just leaves the possibility that he never left."

"Yes, Lowe told me you'd been through the footage. I understand you identified one of the cars. Thank you for that." It was a begrudging thanks.

"Did Lowe find out why the Punto was there?"

"Yes, it seems Corby was running errands up to Trivett's. And he ferried his wife back and forth to see Frances Trivett a few times. Giles Trivett was at a conference for a few days and Erin

Colby and Frances Trivett often socialise when he's away. Frances Trivett confirmed it. Corby hadn't thought it important enough to mention."

I said, "What concerns me the most is the message Black left at the surgery. Okay, so I get that he would leave a message rather than call during working hours if he didn't want to be questioned too closely. But why a text message? I don't buy the idea that he didn't want to be overheard. He would have been able to arrange to call in private."

Nathan nodded. "And the one reason that makes sense is so the voice couldn't be identified. Which suggests someone else sent the message. Yes, I guess we're thinking along the same lines."

"And if someone else did send that message, it must have been because they wanted to give the impression there was a legitimate reason for Black's disappearance."

Nathan affirmed his agreement. "Which, in turn suggests that his disappearance is anything but legitimate."

"And another thing. Look around this place." I swept my hand out before me. "This room is disorganised. Newspapers scattered on the floor. A half-full coffee cup on the table. I don't think he would have left the room like this if he had a choice."

"The guy could just be a slob."

"No way. Believe me, Black is a total neat freak. Look at this." I led us to Black's study. "See how precisely everything is arranged in here? This is definitely a sign of obsessiveness. Look at the desk. See how ..." I froze.

"What? What is it?"

"The laptop is missing?"

"Missing?"

"Yes. Last night, there was a laptop on that desk."

"Last night?" His voice rose. "Is there something you need to tell me?" There was a sharp edge to his tone.

I swallowed hard and said, "I took a quick look around last night. Just checked for signs of a break in and took a look through the windows. I was up here anyway. It was no big deal."

He wasn't buying it. "What the fuck does it take to get through to you?"

"Oh, come on. It was just a quick look. Where's the harm in that?"

"Because when I tell you not to interfere, it means don't fucking interfere. It doesn't mean ignore what I tell you and do as you please."

"Okay, I get it. Sorry. But if I hadn't checked around, we wouldn't know the laptop was missing would we?"

"Which is the only reason I don't kick your arse."

"Sorry, I didn't think you'd mind," I lied.

"Remember in future," he said, poking me in the chest, "you're here to give advice in an observational role. Nothing else."

I was saved from any further dressing down by the return of the two constables. Nathan reigned in his temper and turned his attention to them. One of them shook his head. "Nothing up there," he said.

"Okay," Nathan said, "I want this place sealed off. No one to come in or out without my say so. And I want Forensics over here. Fingerprints. Especially around the desk."

The same constable nodded his assent and Nathan and I made our way back to his car.

I said, "Why do you suppose someone would come back for the laptop? Do you think it could have been Black?"

"Who knows." He was curt. Obviously still mad at me and not in a communicative mood.

I braced myself mentally and said, "There's something else maybe I should tell you."

He halted and turned, glaring.

"While I was looking around last night, I think someone else was here." I told him about hearing the gate and finding it opened and about the feeling of being watched.

With a despairing look, he said, "Does it never occur to you that you might be putting yourself in harm's way?"

"Don't worry. I won't be wandering around up here on my

own any time soon."

"Believe me, you'd better not be or I'll make your life a misery."

I held up my hands in an attitude of surrender. "Whatever you say. I'll just get back to the vicarage and stay out of your way."

I turned and beat a hasty retreat before he could unleash any more threats. I could feel his eyes burning into my back as I left.

CHAPTER TWENTY-SEVEN

Lowe arrived at the vicarage in the early evening to pick up Karen and I waved them off, telling them I would stay for a while longer.

I picked up the pile of papers from the dining table and rifled through them. Most of them were of no value; old drafts of sermons, scribbled aide memoirs, even receipts that were several years old. It seemed my father was a hoarder. I carried the papers into the study, and settled down at the desk to go through them.

The scent of pine air freshener irritated my nostrils and did little to disguise the underlying smell of damp and neglect. But at least that noisome stench had faded. I worked methodically, sorting the papers into two piles; those to be disposed of and others, current receipts, invoices and final demands, that I would need to pass on to my father's executors.

I worked steadily until, job done, I leaned back, arched my back and stretched, freeing the tension in my muscles.

Outside the wind was blowing up again and tendrils of cold air snaked in through gaps in the ill-fitting window casing. My watch told me it was nearly ten. I was hungry and tired. Barwell's house wasn't far, a twenty-minute walk at the most, but I wasn't up to making my way back through the darkness in the squally weather. I could use some of the clean bedding Karen had gathered up and camp out here for the night. Maybe find some cans of food in the larder and make myself a rudimentary meal.

I took some sheets from the dining room and carried them upstairs. The treads groaned underfoot.

My old bedroom was much as I remembered it. The furnishing were sparse and utilitarian; a single bed, a small wardrobe and a side table. It didn't look as if it had been used much since my departure. I made up the bed, stripped off and climbed in, all thought of food forgotten. Sleep came within minutes.

I don't know what it was that woke me. A sound maybe? One moment I was sleeping and the next wide awake, alert, muscles tensed.

The wind slapped at the walls, rattling the windowpanes, and the old house creaked the way old houses do.

But something was wrong.

Among the random external sounds of nature, I was hearing something else. Something rhythmic, deliberate. A series of steady creaks as if someone was walking across the floor.

Downstairs.

I eased myself out of bed, slipped into my jeans and sweatshirt, and crept out onto the balustraded open landing that looked down over the large central hall.

The front door, opposite the foot of the stairs, led out to the covered porch, and doors on the two adjacent walls opened into other rooms.

Moonlight streamed in, filtered through the limbs of an old wind-blown oak outside the window. Shadow branches scraped and clutched at the floor and walls, and dancing patterns of light and dark rippled around the room giving the illusion that it was a living breathing membrane. At school, my English language teacher had once told me I lacked imagination. It was at times like this I wished she'd been right.

I padded down the stairs, senses on high alert.

In the hall, I turned and turned again, peering into the shadows and checking all the corners. Nothing.

Had I imagined it? Was I spooked because I was alone in this old creepy house?

A brass candlestick stood within reach on a side table against the nearest wall. I picked it up and tested its heft in the palm of my other hand. If need be, it would make a useful weapon.

Outside the wind roared and a draught of cold air swept through the open dining room door into the hall. I steeled myself, crossed to the door, and stepped over the threshold into the relative darkness beyond. The French windows leading to the patio at the side of the house were open. Now at least I knew for sure. It wasn't my imagination. Someone else was in the house. A trickle of sweat ran down my back.

I scanned the room.

The drapes, caught by the wind, blew inward, flapping against the open doors. The glass chandelier above the dining table tinkled. Nothing else moved.

Hugging the walls, I crept from the dining room and edged my way around the perimeter of the hall to the kitchen on the far side. I peered around the door frame. Empty. I stepped into the kitchen and checked all the corners for sign of movement. Again, nothing.

The sudden crack of a floorboard behind me.

I whirled around, candlestick raised.

Something struck the side of my head.

I cried out.

A blinding flash of light and pain and the hard wooden floor raced up and slammed into me. For the briefest of moments, a bright red glare filled my vision and then faded to oblivion as consciousness left me.

I'm not sure how long I lay there on the floor between the kitchen and the hall. Long enough for the damp air to seep into my bones and leave me stiff and cold.

Shards of light danced behind my eyes and my head throbbed. I tried to push myself up from the floor and get to my feet but the room was spinning and so I stayed where I was. All around me, papers and clothing were strewn around the floor.

I felt in my pocket. My phone was still there. I called Nathan.

CHAPTER TWENTY-EIGHT

Nathan slammed the Astra into fourth and sped off into the darkness. "Just for once, do as you're Goddamn told," he barked.

"I don't need this. I'm fine."

"I'm taking you to A&E. End of discussion."

I groaned, loudly enough to make sure he got the message.

"You were out cold for several hours, Mikey. And I didn't get up in the middle of the night just to offer you sympathy."

"Okay. Okay." There was no point arguing with him.

The road gleamed wet and icy in the moonlight. Gusts of wind buffeted the car.

He muttered under his breath and said, "Christ. I'd forgotten what a pain you could be when you dug your heels in." He slammed back down into second as we took the turn towards the hospital, taking his temper out on the gearstick.

"Yeah, happy days," I retorted.

He grunted and lapsed into silence.

I took a sideways glance at him. His jaw was set firm. I felt a pang of remorse. "I'm sorry I'm such a pain. I am grateful."

He grunted again. "Who knew you were up at the vicarage?"

"Just you, Lowe and Karen. You're not suggesting this was personal are you?"

"It's possible. You've been interfering with the investigation. Someone might resent that."

"Interfering?"

"You've been asking questions of potential witnesses instead of leaving it to the police. That's called interfering. And you might well have pissed someone off."

I stayed quiet. It probably wasn't the best of times to let him know that I hadn't finished yet. There was at least one more possible witness I intended to talk to. I veered away from the subject. "No one else knew I was there. Whoever trashed the place was looking for something. I'm sure of that. My presence there was just an inconvenient coincidence."

"Maybe. But either way, the vicarage is off limits again. My men are securing the place and I'm sending in a team to check it out."

I grunted an acknowledgement, and we passed the rest of the journey in silence.

A&E was as depressing as expected. There was the usual motley crew that A&E staff were used to seeing at that time in the morning. The ones with the bruised knuckles and bloody noses that followed a drunken night out on the town. Some of the more sober ones who probably still had a fair idea of where they were glared up at Nathan as he passed. Even in plainclothes, a policeman stood out a mile.

"You don't have to stay," I said, as we settled ourselves into a couple of chairs in the waiting area. "I can get the late bus back home."

"Yeah, right. And as soon as I'm on my way, you'll be out of here."

Foiled again. I was going to have to go through with it.

When we eventually saw a doctor, he turned out to be one of those unremittingly cheerful ones that put your teeth on edge. He must have been a newbie. Another few years of this and he'd soon be as worn down and cynical as the rest of his colleagues.

His method of examination was restricted to holding up a single finger and asking me to count them, asking me my name and age, and checking my ability to recall what day it was and the name of the current Prime Minster. I passed with flying colours.

"There are no signs of any underlying injury," the doctor said, brightly. "But we'll keep you in overnight to be on the safe side."

"No." I objected.

"Yes," said Nathan. "And if he causes you any trouble, call me and I'll send someone over to arrest him."

"Oh." The doc didn't sound so sparky now.

"He's joking," I said. "He has a strange sense of humour."

Nathan fixed me with a steely gaze. "Don't be so sure."

I decided not to risk it.

"I'll pick you up in the morning," Nathan said.

"I'll be right here, ready and raring to go."

"Good. You'll need to be. Tomorrow's going to be a busy day. We're going body hunting."

CHAPTER TWENTY-NINE

The weather wasn't any better the following day. But after a sleepless night in the local hospital, the prospect of tramping through Tinkers Woods on a wet and windy day seemed a positive improvement. I was still complaining to Nathan about what I saw as my enforced hospital stay.

"Stop carping," he said. "It's always best to be on the safe side with these things."

"I'd rather have spent a day in prison."

"Don't tempt me."

We were crossing the courtyard at the front of Black's house. A team of four uniformed officers were over at the far side being prepped by Lowe.

He turned to face us as we made our way toward him over the icy paving. His downcast expression suggested all was not well. "We have a problem."

"What now?" Nathan sounded less upbeat than he had a moment ago.

"The dog handler hasn't turned up. It seems they didn't have anyone to spare at the last moment."

"Oh, that's great. So we're just wasting our time."

"Perhaps not. Maybe I could help," I said.

"Really? And just what were you thinking of doing? Getting down on you hands and knees and sniffing around." Nathan was getting snappy.

For one wild moment I considered reminding him that it wouldn't be the first time I'd got down on my hands and knees for him. But sanity kicked in and I decided that maybe discretion was called for. Instead, I said, "It just needs some applied psychology."

Nathan said, "I don't know what you have in mind, but these woods cover a very wide area, and with the best will in the world, I don't think we can do anything useful here without a dog."

"Listen to me for a moment. The woods are too dense to have been driven over from any of the other access points so if our

The Slow Road to Hell

theory is correct and Black is our second murder victim, our hypothetical murderer either walked through the woods or drove along Vicarage Lane. Okay with me so far?"

"As far as it goes, yes."

"We've already concluded that if our murderer did drive here, he's unlikely to have then moved the body by road. Why take the risk when Black's house backs onto convenient secluded woodland?"

I pointed to the gate leading into the woods. "There's no other way into the woods from this side, and with no access for a vehicle from either side, our murderer would have had to move the body on foot. Okay?" I paused for confirmation.

Nathan accepted the point.

"Good. Now come over here." I led the way to the gate.

Nathan, Lowe and the constables followed on behind. The smell of damp earth was strong here.

"Look at the terrain," I said. "It's been raining for weeks. The ground is muddy. And whilst that might mean that any signs of activity have been washed away, it must also have caused problems for our hypothetical murderer, or murderers if there was more than one."

"How does that help us?" asked Lowe.

"You have to try to see the situation from their point of view. They're carrying a dead weight, literally, and whilst they're going to want to dispose of the body as far from the beaten track as possible, they're not going to want to make it too hard on themselves."

Lowe interjected again. "So they won't have gone too far into the woods."

"Exactly. And look how the ground slopes over there." I pointed to a spot in front of us. "Admittedly, it's not much of a slope but look at how muddy and wet it is. Our murderer would have trouble carrying a body that way."

"So he's more likely to have skirted around it," Nathan said.

"Yes. So you should be checking the ground to the left and right around the edge of the slope."

Lowe said, "That still leaves a lot of ground to cover."

Nathan took over. "Well, that's where applied psychology leaves off and basic tracking skills take over. Despite the heavy rains, there's still a covering of leaf mulch on those areas away from the trail. Even if most signs of ground disturbance have been washed away by the rain, the murderer would have had to dig through and destroy the ground cover. So we should be looking for any spots where there's a distinct lack of leaf mulch."

Lowe assented. "We'll split into two groups and take either side of the path. Did you get all of that, guys?"

Satisfied with the expressions of confirmation, he led the way through the gate, split the men into two groups, leading one group to the left and sending the other to the right."

Once they were out of earshot, Nathan said, "Maybe you have your uses after all."

"I'm not saying we'll find anything, but at least it's worth a try. Your men were already here and we have nothing to lose."

"Maybe. But I'm still pissed off about the lack of support from the dog unit. We're always under threat from Government cuts but God knows how we're supposed to do our jobs when basic resources are constantly being depleted. I guess we have to do the best we can. It's a sign of the times."

"As one of my more alliterative friends used to say, 'fucked by the fickle finger of fate'."

Nathan grunted. "It's good to know you have friends who appreciate the higher art forms."

I snorted. "Careful, Nathan, you almost cracked a joke there."

"Purely unintentional I assure you."

Nearby, rain dripped from the trees and splashed to the ground around us.

"I miss this," I said.

"What?"

"The way we used to spark off each other. I miss it." A sense of emptiness and loss swept through me. There was a lump in my throat. "I'll go and wait in the car. No point standing around in the cold." I left him there and hurried over to the Astra.

I sat in the car and stared out in front of me. Rivulets of water ran down the windscreen and rain clattered on the roof.

After all this was over, I would have to start making plans. Another chapter in my life over. Time to start afresh. But I had no real sense of what I wanted and where I was heading. I was so alone.

The driver side door opened and Nathan slid in beside me. "Are you okay?" He sounded puzzled.

I couldn't speak. I nodded, stared straight ahead.

"Something's wrong," he said.

I turned to face him and smiled. "I'm okay. I'm just feeling a bit overwhelmed. The stress of the last few days is catching up with me I guess."

"What will you do when all this is over?"

He must have read my mind. "I wish I knew."

He grunted in response. There was nothing he could say.

"I'll be okay," I said, trying to sound confident.

"Mikey ..." He paused for a moment, as if unsure what to say.

But the moment passed. We were interrupted by a shout from the far side of the courtyard. Lowe stood by the gate, waving his arms in our direction.

Nathan went back into professional mode. "Looks like they've found something." He was out of the car and running towards the woods.

By the time I reached them, Nathan was standing by the partially exposed remains of a decomposing body, barking out orders and clearing the site. It looked as if we had found our man.

CHAPTER THIRTY

The hum of conversation increased as more and more members of the local force entered the room. It was the day after Black's body had been unearthed and we were back in the large meeting room at the rear of Elders Edge Police Station. Nathan, Lowe and I sat facing two rows of metal-framed chairs which gradually filled as the assembled group of police officers seated themselves. I got a few disconcerting looks. No doubt my current starring role in the media had been the subject of much lurid gossip and my presence here would raise a few eyebrows.

Once everyone was in place, Nathan opened the meeting and the conversation died down.

"Most of you guys are well acquainted with this investigation," he said, "but for the benefit of those of you who've just joined us, I'll go over what we have so far."

He brought the group up to date on the current situation; two murders within a few days of each other, cause of death being the same in both cases.

After appraising the group of the possible theft of the laptop from Black's place and the break-in at the vicarage, he admitted that the investigating team had failed to find any useful evidence and it was still unclear if either incident was connected to the murders.

He said, "We've not been able to establish a motive or a clear link between the victims but the Medical Examiner's report shows that both died in a similar manner. In Black's case, there were other injuries, blunt force trauma consistent with a beating but the actual cause of death in both cases was strangulation."

A uniformed officer on the front row interrupted. "Do we know if the two victims were known to each other?"

"We've been unable to establish a close personal tie between the two men," said Nathan. "But we do know that they met and had some sort of disagreement before they were murdered."

Someone else asked, "Have we been able to establish the exact time of death? Were they killed at the same time?"

"We don't yet have a clear idea of the timing. But from witness evidence, we've been able to establish when they were both last seen - or rather last heard - alive. As that was in the last few days, we can say for sure that both deaths occurred, if not at the same time, within a short time of each other."

Lowe took over. "In view of the new developments, we're going to re-interview all those who knew both Owen MacGregor and Malcolm Black. That will include family members and work colleagues. And we'll be looking for connections between the two."

Nathan confirmed his Sergeant's directive and said, "And that's where Mr MacGregor here comes in." He tilted his head in my direction. "Most of you will know Michael MacGregor as Owen MacGregor's son. However, he's here today in his professional capacity as a forensic psychologist. I've asked him to appraise our witness statements and sit in on future interviews. Mr MacGregor has experience in this field and has been of some professional assistance to other police forces in the UK."

I affirmed this and said, "I'm sure you'll all appreciate that I'm as eager as anyone here to track down my father's murderer. I'll be glad to give whatever assistance I can."

Someone at the back called out, "Is Mr MacGregor sure he can give the investigation his full attention given all his current problems?"

A ripple of laughter ran around the room. Nathan shuffled in his chair.

I smiled and said, "Having a close relative murdered tends to focus your attention remarkably well." The laughter died. Touché.

Lowe took over again and allocated each of the assembled group to their working teams and outlined their respective duties, including more house to house enquiries for the uniforms and interviews of family, friends and colleagues for the plainclothes.

During this assignment process my mobile buzzed. It was Karen. She knew I was taking part in this meeting so it must have been something that couldn't wait.

I leaned over to Nathan and whispered, "I need to take this."

The meeting was coming to a close anyway and I wouldn't be needed so I left the room, answered the call, and closed the door behind me.

"I have Erin Corby here," Karen said. "She wanted to speak to you and I wasn't sure if I should tell her you'd moved out."

"Keep her there," I said. "The meeting is finishing now so I'll come on over. I'll be no more than a minute or so."

I finished the call as the door opened. The assorted team members filed out in small groups, chatting amiably. I stepped back and waited for Lowe to appear. He and Nathan came out together. I told them where I was going and that I would get in touch later to discuss future developments. We agreed to meet that afternoon and Nathan excused himself and returned to his office. I put a restraining hand on Lowe's arm and once Nathan was out of earshot, I asked him about his follow-up enquiries on Adam Corby's journeys to and from Vicarage Lane.

"You say you spoke to Adam Corby," I said, "but did Erin confirm what he said?"

Lowe scratched his head. "Not that I recall. I was satisfied with his explanation and didn't see any need to question it further."

I murmured an acknowledgement.

"Besides," he continued, "I spoke with Giles Trivett later that day, and Frances Trivett confirmed his explanation. Why do you ask?"

"No reason. I'm on my way to meet Erin and it crossed my mind."

Lowe raised his brows. He was puzzled, but I wasn't about to enlighten him yet. I needed to check out something first.

As I crossed the reception toward the main entrance, Nathan appeared from his office and stopped me. "I've had confirmation that your father's body has been released. So you can go ahead and make arrangements for the funeral."

I nodded my acknowledgement, and he went on, "I'm sorry about that quip in the meeting. I'll let the team know that sort of behaviour is not acceptable."

"Oh please. There's no need. It's just a nine-day wonder. That's something I'm going to have to get used to until the heat dies down."

Jibes at my expense were the least of my concerns right now.

CHAPTER THIRTY-ONE

Karen and Erin were seated around the gas fire in Karen's private sitting room, chatting over cups of coffee. Karen made her excuses when I arrived, vanishing into reception, and I settled myself into the armchair she had just vacated.

Erin put her empty cup on the small occasional table. "Sorry about turning up like this. But you said you were staying here, and I wanted to return this." She reached down to a handbag at the side of her chair and produced my mother's bracelet.

I took it from her with grateful thanks. "I hope I've not made things difficult for you," I said.

Erin pulled a wry face. "Someone has to look out for the child. Her dad's not doing so well."

I pocketed the bracelet. "It must be hard for him too."

"It's not easy for a man like him having to raise a teenage daughter. But he can be a bit strict at times."

"I'm sure you do what you can."

"I do my best. And I'm ever so grateful to you for not going to the police. You would have been entitled."

I dismissed her thanks. "I know it must be hard for the child. And I wouldn't want to add to the family's problems in the circumstances." As an afterthought, I asked, "Does her father know about this?"

"No. I thought it best not to tell him." More emphatically, she added, "But I'll not go easy on her. There'll be big trouble if she tries something like this again. And I'll be keeping a close eye on her from now on."

"I'm happy to leave it to you," I said, and added, "Counselling isn't my particular field of expertise but, even so, if I can ever be of any help, just ask."

Erin thanked me. "I'll bear it in mind. But you have troubles enough of your own at the moment." She gestured toward a folded newspaper lying on the table. "The sort of nonsense these papers dream up is disgraceful."

I pulled a face and said, "It's a consequence of being in the public eye." I was happy to let her go on thinking it was nonsense.

As if on cue, the sound of laughter carried through from the reception and we both glanced towards the door.

Erin said, "They're still here. Those reporters. Asking lots of questions."

"They'll soon find something else to write about and move on."

"I shouldn't think they'll be leaving soon," she said. "Not after this terrible news about Dr Black. Everyone is talking about it. It makes you wonder if it's safe to walk the streets. Things like that don't happen in a place like this."

"Did you know Dr Black?"

"Everyone knew Dr Black. A lovely man. He was our doctor. And I cleaned for him so I got to know him quite well."

"I hadn't realised. It must be particularly upsetting for you, knowing both victims."

Erin grimaced. "No more than anyone else. In a small place like this you get to know most people."

"Did Dr Black and my father know each other? I mean, did they socialise at all?"

"Not that I know of. I never saw them together and neither of them ever said anything to suggest it. But then Dr Black was never one for mixing. Kept himself to himself. I used to feel sorry for him. All alone in that big house. But it was his choice I suppose."

She reached down to the side of her chair, picked up her bag and stood up. "I mustn't keep you any longer. I'm sure you have a lot to do."

I stood and patted my pocket. "Thanks again for this."

I walked her to the door, and we said our goodbyes. As she was about to leave, I said, " I suppose you must get to know a lot of the local people in your line of work."

"I suppose so."

"Do you work for the Trivetts?"

"They don't need any help. Frances is the domestic type."

"She's a friend of yours, isn't she?"

"We've known each other for years. I've not seen much of her recently though."

"Really? I understood you often kept each other company when Giles was away."

"We did, yes. But she's been busy helping Giles with parish matters over the past few weeks so we've not had time to catch up."

It seemed my suspicions were correct after all. I let Erin go, closed the door behind her, and made my way back to my chair.

I was deep in thought when Karen returned.

"You look very serious," she said. "Is everything okay?"

I said, "One of the witnesses is lying."

CHAPTER THIRTY-TWO

We were on our way to the funeral. Nathan was driving. As usual, we were arguing.

Nathan said, "You have to be joking."

I was trying to convince him of my suspicions about Adam Corby and Frances Trivett. But he was having none of it.

"I'm telling you," I said, "They're having an affair."

"And you base this fanciful claim on what? A few car trips to and from Vicarage Lane?"

I'd already told him what I'd seen on the CCTV footage. "There was a pattern. Every time Giles Trivett left for the day, Alan Corby's car came and went twice before Trivett returned."

"So?"

"So I reckon he was picking up Frances for the day and then driving her back home before Giles returned."

"You have an overactive imagination."

"Yes, well I can remember many occasions when you had good cause to appreciate my active imagination."

"What do you ...? Oh." There was embarrassment in his voice. "Irrelevant," he said.

We drove on in silence for a while.

It was a good day for the funeral. That's if there ever is a good day for funerals. A light rain was falling but at least the bitter cutting wind had died away at last.

Nathan spoke up again. "And besides, Lowe checked it out. Corby was taking his wife over to see Frances Trivett."

"An explanation given by Adam Corby and which Frances Trivett later confirmed."

"Exactly."

"Exactly. Only problem is the one person Lowe didn't bother to check with, Erin Corby, doesn't seem to be aware that her husband was giving her lifts. I asked her. She claims not to have seen Frances for some time. Which means Adam Corby and Frances Trivett are lying."

Nathan still wasn't convinced. "It doesn't make sense. It

would be such an obvious lie to disprove. Maybe you got it wrong. Or Erin did."

"No way. And Adam Corby would have said the first thing that came into his head and hoped for the best. People don't always think things through when they're put on the spot. Right now, they're probably worried about being exposed."

We turned into Vicarage Lane and parked up opposite the gateway into the courtyard.

As we climbed out of the car, I said, "It would be easy enough to check. Just interview Erin Corby and check her story against theirs. They'll soon come clean when confronted with the truth."

Nathan unfurled an umbrella and held it over us as we made our way across the courtyard towards the church at the back of the vicarage. He said, "Is that a good idea? If they are having an affair - and I'm not saying they are - whatever lies they're telling are to cover up their own indiscretions. Nothing to do with our investigation. So is it worth stirring things up?"

"We can't ignore it. It has an impact on the investigation."

"How so?"

"Jonas Wainwright wasn't certain who my father argued with before he was killed. He thought maybe it was Black but he wasn't absolutely sure. Okay?"

"So far. Go on."

"It was only when Frances confirmed his belief that we all presumed it must have been Black after all. But suppose she's lying and she wasn't even there. Without her corroboration, it was just a possibility of it being Black. But now we're taking it as a given."

"Are you suggesting it was someone else?"

We had almost reached the entrance to the church where Giles Trivett, dressed in white vestments, stood with a small group of mourners. Karen was with them and before I could reply to Nathan in any detail, she broke away and came over to join us.

"We'll talk later," I said.

We reached the rest of the group and condolences were exchanged. Once the coffin arrived, carried over from the vicarage by four pall bearers, Trivett led it into the church and we all followed on behind.

Karen clung to my arm as we made our way to the front of the nave and took our places in the first pew. Quite a crowd flocked into the church. Was I being cynical or were they here to take vicarious pleasure in a local drama?

Some of the faces I recognised. Adam Corby and Frances Trivett sat together. No surprise there. I'd already heard that Erin was looking after Laura while her father attended the funeral. He hadn't thought she would be up to it. Jonas Wainwright seated himself next to them.

And, of course, the Press were in full attendance; Jeff Stokes from the local rag, and Brian Driscoll and the sleazeball John Chesterton from the Nationals. They sat in a group at the back of the church like a bad stain on a clean floor. Lowe was here too and I recognised some of the officers I'd recently faced at the police conference.

I sat through the tribute and prayers in a half-trance, not taking it in and when Trivett read out a prayer for forgiveness, I had to wonder who was being forgiven and why.

I was relieved when the service was over and I could get back into the open air, out from under the oppressive weight of those ancient stones.

At the graveside, a few tears were shed as the coffin was lowered into the grave. That surprised me. I was my father's closest relative and yet I felt nothing, just a numbness. I tried to conjure up some memory of our times together, something to take comfort from, a reminder of happier times. But nothing came.

Karen squeezed my hand. Nathan stood on my other side, holding his umbrella over the three of us. My spirits lifted. I was grateful to have them near.

Once the burial was over, I made a point of circulating to thank people for attending and was on my way back over to Nathan and Karen when a hand clasped my arm. It was Jonas Wainwright, looking decidedly embarrassed.

"I hope you don't mind me asking," he said. "I know this

might not be the best of times ..."

"Hey, life goes on," I said, trying not to sound too flippant.

"The thing is, I was in the middle of carrying out some work for your father before, you know ..." he waved his hand around, "before all this."

"Before he died, yes."

Wainwright's embarrassment increased. "Yes. I was expecting to return to finish off and left my toolbox over there."

"And, of course, you want it back."

"I'd be happy to go over there and get it myself. And I could finish off the repairs I started. No charge of course."

"That's kind of you but I'm sure there's no need." I was touched by his generosity. He must have valued my father's help and guidance a great deal. "And besides," I continued, "the vicarage is off limits at the moment. The police haven't finished there yet."

Wainwright looked disappointed, so I took his number and offered to get the toolbox back to him as soon as possible. He accepted the offer but still didn't look too happy about it.

I left him and hurried after Nathan and Karen. Together, we walked over to the cars and arranged to meet at the Fairview.

Back in the car, Nathan said, "I've been thinking over what you said. About Frances Trivett."

"And what did you come up with?"

"It occurs to me that if she had chosen to lie, she wouldn't have needed to back up Wainwright's claim. She could just as easily have said she was away from home. Shopping or whatever. So, given that she did corroborate what Wainwright told us, doesn't that suggest she's telling the truth?"

"She may have already told Giles she was at home and once she'd told the lie, she would have to run with it. Otherwise, he may have become suspicious."

Nathan grunted and lapsed into silence as we turned into the Esplanade and made our way towards the Fairview. He must have been thinking it over. "Bit of a coincidence though, isn't it? We're given every reason to believe he was the last to see your father alive and then he turns up dead. Seems pretty certain to me."

I shrugged. "Maybe," I said, "but I think it's worth re-interviewing her. If she is lying, it opens up the possibility of alternative lines of enquiry to follow."

We pulled into the car park behind the Fairview and drew up opposite the rear entrance.

Nathan said, "We're re-interviewing everyone anyway."

We crossed the car park towards the door and I said, "I'd like to sit in on her interview if that's okay."

"Sure. I'll let you know once it's been arranged. But I'm not convinced it will make any difference."

I left it at that.

Karen had prepared a buffet in the bar for some of the mourners and had closed it to the public. John Chesterton and a number of other reporters tried to blag their way in but were turned away. Disgruntled, they left the Fairview, presumably seeking out an alternative watering hole.

People stood around talking in hushed whispers. I was edgy, eager to get away.

I said to Nathan, "I wonder if anyone would notice if I sneaked off."

"Probably. And it wouldn't look too good. Bad form."

"Like that's ever bothered me," I said. But I stayed anyway.

Giles Trivett arrived about a quarter of an hour later wearing a change of clothes, a grey suit and black armband. Adam Corby and Frances Trivett had been talking together before he arrived but now they drifted apart and mingled with the other mourners.

I managed to catch Trivett's attention once he'd finished speaking with members of his congregation. "This may not be an appropriate time but I need to discuss my father's estate. I take it you're aware you've been appointed one of his executors?"

He flushed, stammered and said, "Yes, your father sought my consent some time ago."

He must have wondered why my father had chosen not to appoint his only son as his executor. But perhaps he did know. Perhaps my father had told him of his reasons and that's why

Trivett was embarrassed.

I let him know that I had collected and collated all the documents I'd found amongst my father's personal effects and that I would be happy to continue doing so and bring them over to him once I'd finished so he could pass them on to the solicitors.

He agreed to this enthusiastically. "I'm more than happy to let you continue. And I'm grateful for your help."

That settled, I changed the subject, trying to make it sound as if it was a casual enquiry. "You told me Frances didn't recognise whoever it was my father argued with. And yet she later changed her mind. Why was that?"

"We discussed it later. I thought it odd that she wouldn't recognise the voice if it was him. We both know him well and he has such a distinctive voice. She told me she was pretty certain it was Black."

"So why didn't she say so when the police interviewed her."

Trivett glanced over to where Nathan was chatting with Lowe and, lowering his voice, he said, "I know it was silly of her. But she was being over cautious. She didn't want to cause him any trouble and then find out later she was mistaken after all. I persuaded her to go back to the police and change her statement. They were very understanding."

So I was right. She changed her mind after pressure from her husband. More than ever I was sure she was lying.

Trivett kept me talking a while longer. Regaling me with stories of my father and their work together. I listened politely and nodded occasionally, eager to get away, but feeling obliged to stay and hear him out.

Eventually, I was rescued by Karen. "Sorry to butt in but I need Mikey's help with something," she told Trivett.

As she led me away, she whispered, "You looked like you needed an excuse to get away. Giles can be a bit of an old woman when he gets going."

I thanked her and signalled to Nathan that I was ready to leave. He exchanged a few words with Lowe and came over to join us. "I guess we can go now without upsetting anyone. I'll drive you back home. It's been a busy day. I'm sure you must want some time to relax."

"I've got a much better idea," I said. "Why don't you stay for dinner? You can help me unwind. And I promise not to talk about the investigation. I could use some company right now."

He hesitated for the briefest of moments and said, "Sure. Why not? We could both do with some down time."

CHAPTER THIRTY-THREE

Nathan carried our glasses through to the living area and I finished clearing the table.

"You make a mean pasta bake," he said. "I'd forgotten how good home cooking could be."

I grinned and followed him through. "And I'd forgotten what a healthy appetite you had. It was a pleasure to watch you eat it."

Dinner had been a good idea. A pleasant respite from the stress of the past few days. And, by mutual consent, no talk of the ongoing investigation. We'd caught up on the current whereabouts and circumstances of old friends, put the state of the world to rights, and lamented on the recent downturn in the fortunes of Charwell FC, the local football team. The one subject I hadn't made any headway on was Nathan's personal life. Not that I'd pushed too hard but he hadn't been very forthcoming either.

I topped up our glasses while he rummaged through the CD rack. He seemed to know his way around the house quite well. How well I wondered.

"You seem to have settled in okay," he said, looking around the room.

By 'settled in', I presumed he was referring to the way I had strewn my clothing and personal effects around the place.

"I'm just grateful for somewhere to call home for a while." I placed his glass on the cabinet beside him. "I'm very much obliged to your friend."

"He's a very obliging sort of person."

How obliging was something else I wondered about. "How long have you known him?"

"Almost three years." He dropped a Rodrigo disc into the player and adjusted the volume. The spirited sound of the Concierto de Aranjuez filled the room.

"And do you stay here often," I asked.

He looked up sharply. A little too sharply. Obviously, my subtle probing into his personal life wasn't as subtle as I had intended. I turned my attention to the CD case on top of the cabinet, pretending to read its cover.

"Why do you ask?"

Trying to appear nonchalant, I shrugged, made my way over to the couch and settled down on the far side of it. "Just wondered. You seem so much at home." I leaned back and drank some wine.

He picked up his glass from the top of the cabinet, followed me over and dropped onto the other side of the couch. "We're not heavily involved if that's what you want to know. We're just good friends."

"So there's no one special?"

"In my line of work, you don't get a lot of time for relationships."

"You must get some time to socialise."

"I have my moments but nothing serious."

His expression was as impenetrable as ever. He wasn't going to give anything away. So I let it drop.

"What about you?" He said.

"Me?" I snorted. "You need to ask? Don't you read the papers?"

"That's not what I was asking. I mean, where do you go from here? You must have some plans."

"I have a messy - and, I suspect, very public - divorce to get through first. It's best if I sort out my past before planning for the future."

"Will you stay in London?"

Right now, I was relaxed and comfortable, and the last thing I wanted to think about was the future. I fetched the bottle of Merlot from the sideboard while I thought over his question. "I don't yet know what I'm going to do. Maybe I need to get away from London. A change of pace." I replenished my glass, sat back down and leaned over to refill his.

He placed a hand over his glass. "I'd best not. I have a long drive ahead of me."

"Oh, come on, Nathan. Chill out. You deserve a break. And

you don't have to go back tonight. Why don't you stay over? We can make you up a bed in the spare room."

He looked down at his half-empty glass of wine, glanced up at the wall clock above the mantelpiece, and back down to his wine.

"I guess it wouldn't do any harm," he said eventually. "I can always drive back in the morning. If you're sure you wouldn't mind?"

"Mind? Why would I mind?" He moved his hand and I refilled his glass. "I'm enjoying this. Good music, good wine, good company, and no talk of work. What more could I ask for?" I placed the bottle down by the hearth and raised my glass to him.

He raised his in turn and smiled. "In that case, I'm happy to stay."

"Good," I said, pushing myself up off the couch and crossing over to the kitchen unit. "In that case, I'll open another bottle."

"Hey, don't go overboard," he called out.

"Relax. You're not on duty now." I opened another bottle of Merlot, shook a large pack of crisps into a bowl, carried them back to the couch, and placed them on the floor between us.

I dropped back onto the couch and we lapsed into a comfortable silence, the only sound that of Rodrigo's plaintive adagio. I leaned back, eyes closed, enjoying the music while Nathan drank his wine.

Nathan chuckled. I opened one eye. He was smiling.

"What is it?" I said.

"It's good to see you relaxed. You've been on edge these past few days."

"No kidding. I wonder why." I smiled back.

I don't know what made me do it, maybe it was the wine and the mood and the music, but on an impulse, without stopping to think, I leaned towards him and, with a hand against his shoulder, pressed my lips to his.

Nathan tensed. Then pulled back and stared at me, confusion written large on his face.

I moved away and raised a hand between us as if to ward off whatever negative reaction I had provoked.

"I'm sorry," I said. "That was so dumb. I don't know what made me do that. It was the wine I guess. I wasn't thinking." I babbled excuses, embarrassed, trying to explain the inexplicable. "I didn't mean anything by it, I promise you. It was nothing."

Even as I said it, I recognised it for the lie it was. Nothing? That was a joke. Far from being nothing, it had been one of those profound moments when, in a sudden flash of clarity, everything I'd been in denial about became clear. All that angst and soul searching about where I was going and what I wanted. I knew exactly what I wanted. I wanted him. The man I loved.

And with that same dawning realisation came the understanding that those feelings, repressed for so long, had resurfaced too late. I wanted to tell him how I felt. But I couldn't. The look on his face told me all I needed to know about how pointless that would be. And so I looked for excuses instead.

I tried to laugh it off. "Maybe I'd better stay off the wine before I do something else stupid."

A short sharp laugh from Nathan. Not very convincing. He squirmed in his seat, ill at ease and, a moment later, looked up at the clock again and said, "Perhaps it would be best if I went home after all. It's going to be a long day tomorrow."

My heart sank. Why did I have to make such a mess of things when all was going well.

"I'm not sure that's such a good idea, Nathan." I nodded toward the glass of wine in his hand. "You'll be over the limit by now."

He took a moment and then agreed that it probably wouldn't be a wise move and said, "I should turn in anyway. I'll need to make an early start in the morning." He placed his half-full glass down by the hearth.

It was barely ten o'clock, hardly late, but I acquiesced anyway, inwardly cursing myself for the idiot I was and for driving him away. I rose from my seat as he did, and bade him good night as he mounted the stairs.

Trying to sound casual, I called up after him, "There's some bedding in the bedside chest. Do you need a hand?"

"No, I'll be fine, he said, a tad too quickly, and, a moment later, closed the bedroom door behind him.

As the mournful sound of Rodrigo's Fantasia died away, I sank back onto the couch, head in hands, and waited until all sounds of movement from above had ceased. For a minute or two longer, I sat in silence and then took one last look around the empty room before climbing the stairs to bed.

CHAPTER THIRTY-FOUR

Half an hour later, I was still sitting in my bedside chair, wide awake.

All around me, the old house groaned and creaked as it settled down for the night. Floorboards squeaked on the upper landing and from somewhere downstairs, the faint rattle of a radiator presaged the long drawn-out gurgling of water as it coursed its way around the pipes.

In the spare room next door, all was quiet. Was Nathan already sleeping or, like me, was he too restless, fretting about what the hell had just happened?

Was I really so stupid? That I couldn't see what was right in front of me all this time? And more to the point, what was I going to do about it?

Whilst I was reflecting on these thoughts, another sound joined the others; the creak of a door hinge from the corridor outside. It was followed by the soft tread of feet on the wooden floor.

That was one question answered at least. Nathan was still up and about.

The sounds of movement stopped outside my door and I waited, apprehensive, unsure why he was there, wondering if he was about to knock, worried that he might, and ready to be disappointed if he didn't.

A brief pause and he withdrew again.

I was out of my chair in a flash and opened the door in time to see him retreating into his room. He was still dressed.

"Nathan?"

He stopped, half turning, hesitant, uncertain, and then turned around and made his way to me.

He said, "Just tell me if I'm reading this all wrong, Mikey. Am I making a big mistake here?"

A slow shake of the head. "I'm the one who makes all the mistakes." I stepped back to let him into the room. "You're the one who always puts them right again."

A moment later, I was in his arms, holding him tight, his lips pressed to mine. This is where I wanted to be more than anywhere. Where I belonged. Wrapped in those strong arms. Breathing in that heady scent.

And this time there were no excuses, I knew what I wanted. And so did he. He was already unbuttoning his shirt, as ready for this as I was.

He pulled away from me, still tugging at his buttons, and before he could act or speak, I pushed him down onto the bed. He swung himself around to lie full length and I climbed onto the bed and straddled him, swiping away his hand.

"Oh no you don't," I said, my breathing ragged. "I get to unwrap my own presents."

"Is that what I am?"

"You're my welcome home gift."

"Home?"

"You know what I mean."

He kicked off his shoes and I fumbled with the rest of his shirt buttons, his chest heaving and falling under my touch.

Gripping him between my thighs, I ripped open his shirt to reveal the thick mat of hair that covered his torso. I ran my fingers through it, making my way down over the firm pecs to the swirl of hair on the flat plane of his stomach and on to the treasure trail running down under the top of his trousers.

Trying to keep the tremor out of my voice, I said, "I have to say, you've filled out nicely over the years, Mr Quarryman." My cock strained against the fabric of my jeans as I feasted on the sight of that hard hot body and rippling muscles. "I always did have good taste in men."

"Now let's see what I'm getting, shall we, Mr MacGregor?" His voice was husky, deep in the back of his throat. He grabbed the hem of my sweatshirt and dragged it over my head in one fluid movement, pulling my arms up over my head as he tugged it off and threw it aside. "Not bad." His broad hands were all over me, squeezing my arms and pecs. The muscles in his arms rippled beneath the dark covering of hair.

"Not bad?" My voice trembled. "I'll have you know this body cost me a fortune in gym fees."

"Don't worry. You got your money's worth."

"You approve?"

"Oh, I approve all right." He grabbed me around the waist and half pushed, half pulled me over onto the middle of the bed, rolled over, wrapped a muscular leg around my thighs, and leaned down, seeking my lips once more. He pushed his tongue into my mouth and I took it in eagerly, wrapping my own tongue around his, enjoying the wine-tangy taste of him. His bristles scraped my skin as he pressed his mouth hard against mine.

I pulled away, gulping in air. "Wait. Wait a moment." I rolled him onto his back again and reached for his belt.

The next few minutes were lost in a frenzy of activity, of belts unbuckled and zips undone, and a whir of flying clothes as jeans, trousers, shirts and underwear were ripped off and cast aside. And then Nathan was reaching over to the bedside cabinet, wrenching open the drawer and grabbing a tube of lube.

"On top," he barked. I straddled him again and a second later, he was guiding his finger to its target. As he found his mark, I relaxed enough to let his lube-slick finger slide into me, threw back my head and cried out. Beneath me, his thick cock throbbed and jerked, pressing into me. My heart raced.

"I need you," I moaned.

Leaning down, I squeezed his pecs, digging my fingers into his hairy pelt, and ground my hips, writhing against his swollen cock. His flesh was warm and damp. Beads of sweat broke out on his forehead and he groaned, gripping me around the waist and bucking his hips, pressing into me.

"The drawer. The drawer. A condom." His arm outstretched, he was grabbing thin air as he tried to reach the drawer handle. I beat him to it, almost ripped the drawer off its runners in my haste and rummaged around inside it until I found what I was looking for.

He tried to snatch it from me but I held it out of his reach. "I'll do it," I said, tearing it out of its wrapper. "I want to take a good look at what I've been missing."

I swung myself off his lap and reached down to grab the thick rampant cock as it sprang free, and ran the thumb of my free hand up and down the thick vein on the underside of his shaft. The glans was slick with pre-cum and, moaning with pleasure, I leaned down and pressed my lips to the large bulbous head, ran my tongue over the glistening drop of pre-cum leaking from the tip of his cock, enjoying the salty taste, and then took it into my mouth, greedily sucking it down into the back of my throat, running my tongue around the shaft.

Nathan groaned, writhing beneath me, his fingers curled into my hair. He pulled me down, grinding his hips, and forced his cock into the back of my throat.

Pulling back, I released him and raised my head. "Seems such a shame to cover it up." My heart was racing.

"Well, you'd best do it soon" He was panting hard as he released his hold on me. "Or you'll be getting a facial."

"Hmmm, promises, promises." I unrolled the condom onto his shaft and waited till he'd lubed up before straddling him again. Reaching behind me, I grasped his cock and guided it into place. He grunted and slowly pushed into me.

"Easy, boy. Easy," I said. "It's been a while since I had one this size."

He slid into me, taking his time, and, as the discomfort passed and I relaxed, he gradually increased his stroke until he was pounding hard, slamming his thick member deep into me. I bucked and thrashed, pushing back to meet each thrust. He drove into me, the fingers of one hand digging into the cheeks of my ass, the other hand wrapped around my shaft, pumping slowly as our guttural groans drowned out the complaining squeak of the bedsprings.

As my moment neared, my balls tightened and the juices rose in my shaft. From somewhere far away, I heard myself cry out, a long high wailing sound as the world exploded in a paroxysm of pleasure, and fire raged through my flesh.

The world came back into focus, and I heard Nathan's

rumbling shout of release as he filled me with his juices. A moment later I collapsed, sobbing and shaking, onto his chest as he withdrew.

Gently, he rolled me onto my side and wrapped an arm around me. We lay together in silence, spent and satiated, our sweat-warm bodies pressed together, his heart beating against my skin, my hand on his chest.

After long moments of silence, he said, "Is this a game changer, Mikey?"

I didn't want to think about the future. "I just want to enjoy this moment. The future can take care of itself."

That night, for the first time in many nights, I slept soundly. I must have. Because when I woke the following morning, Nathan had already gone.

CHAPTER THIRTY-FIVE

Chin in hand, my head propped up on one arm, I shoved the food around my plate, occasionally stabbing at a sausage or piece of bacon with my fork as my breakfast congealed. My appetite had gone.

I occasionally glanced over to the chair on the other side of the kitchen table where Nathan should have been sitting. It was empty. And I wasn't sure why.

Last night, everything had changed. All those pent-up emotions I had suppressed for so long had finally surfaced into awareness, throwing me into confusion about what I was looking for, about my feelings for Nathan, about how it would change our relationship.

It was as if the ground beneath me had given way and I was being pulled down into a quagmire of bewildering possibilities, left struggling to find my feet again, wondering what happened now and where we went from here. So many questions. And Nathan was the only one who could help me answer them.

So where was he? Why had he left my bed in the early hours and crept away?

And why wasn't he answering my calls?

My mobile sat on the table by my plate, its face black and sullen. I willed it to ring. One call, two texts, and fifty minutes later, I was still sat there, toying with my food, waiting for him to get back to me.

I picked up the phone, turned it over and over in my hand, started to tap in his number, stopped, put it back down.

Finally, defeated, I dragged myself to the kitchen unit and tipped the remains of my breakfast into the waste-bin.

I couldn't face it any longer.

In that dismal silence, the sound of the doorbell was an ear-shattering shock that had me dropping my cutlery into the sink with a clatter.

Rushing towards the door, I almost fell over a kitchen chair. It had to be Nathan. He must have been called away and now he was back. Why he didn't use his key?

I soon had my answer. It wasn't him.

"Are you okay?"

I'm not sure what it was Lowe read in my face but judging by the look on his, I must have seemed less than welcoming.

"I'm sorry," I stepped back to let him in. "I'm on my first mug of coffee and I'm not totally human till I've had at least three."

He accepted the explanation readily enough and said, "I can come back later if you'd rather."

"No, please." I ushered him in. I was eager for information about Nathan and if Lowe had come straight from the station, he may know what was keeping Nathan so busy he couldn't return my calls.

"Time for a coffee?" I asked.

He accepted, gratefully, rubbing his hands, and sat himself at the kitchen table while I switched on the kettle and spooned some instant into a couple of mugs.

"I wanted to bring you up to speed on the vicarage break-in," he said.

"There've been some developments?"

"'Fraid not. I just wanted to let you know we've finished over there. You're free to go back whenever you like. Sorry to have to tell you though, we didn't find anything of significance."

He must have noticed the look of disappointment on my face as I carried the mugs to the table, and added by way of apology, "I'm sure you'll appreciate that resources are stretched at the moment. In the circumstances, the break-in has to take a lower priority. Particularly as it appears nothing was stolen."

Personally, I thought my being bashed over the head made it a slightly more pressing concern. But I kept my thoughts to myself.

I handed him his coffee and settled myself into the other chair. "And the murder investigations? I'm presuming something's happening there. I've been trying to get hold of Nathan all morning but he seems suddenly very busy."

Lowe's forehead creased. "There's nothing new that I know of. I'm busy arranging more interviews but until we get started on those, the Chief is just catching up on routine work in his office as far as I know."

"Great." My suspicions were confirmed. Nathan was avoiding me.

Lowe studied me, a quizzical look on his face. "Are you sure you're okay?"

I must have spoken more abruptly than I'd intended. "Ignore me. I'm out of sorts."

"Bad night?"

"I wish I knew."

That quizzical look again.

"Let's just say it was some time before I managed to get to sleep." I took a swig of coffee.

Lowe nodded sagely and launched into a discourse on the benefits of regular exercise as a cure for insomnia. I didn't have the heart to tell him that it was a bout of enthusiastic late-night exercise that had kept me from sleeping in the first place.

I half listened to him, responding on automatic with a nod or a smile at convenient moments but my mind was elsewhere. What the hell was Nathan playing at? Last night had been some sort of turning point. What else was it supposed to be? His way of finding closure?

What had it meant to him? In my usual self-centred way, I'd assumed he felt the same. But why would he? Wasn't he the one who'd said he was no good at relationships? The inference being that he wasn't looking for one. So maybe he was running shy. Keeping his distance.

There was something he'd said. Afterwards. Right before I'd fallen asleep. He'd asked me if it had been a game changer. Is that what he was worried about? That I might want more than what was on offer last night? Is that why he'd crept away before I was awake?

There was another possibility. After the revelations about my private life, he may be wary of getting involved with someone he thought lacked commitment. My heart sank. I hoped not. I hoped I hadn't made such a mess of things, I couldn't find some way to redeem myself and make amends for my mistakes.

On the other hand, maybe he really was very busy and I was being paranoid. Maybe I was letting my own guilty conscience persuade me to think the worst. Perhaps that was it. I held on to that thought. It was more comforting than the alternatives.

"Mr MacGregor?"

I came to with a start. Blinked. I hadn't heard a word Lowe had said for the last couple of minutes.

I apologised. "I'm finding it hard to focus right now. Give me that again would you."

He drained his mug and put it down on the table. "I said I'll let you know when I have some interviews arranged. The Chief tells me you want to sit in on them."

"Yes," I said, turning my attention back to our discussion. I needed to concentrate. "Let me know who and when and I'll work around whatever arrangements you make."

I finished my coffee while he produced a pad and pencil from an inside pocket, scribbled a note, and pocketed them again.

With nothing more to discuss, he made his excuses to leave and as he rose from the table, he nodded down at my empty mug and said, "I think you need a few more of those before you're ready to face the world."

CHAPTER THIRTY-SIX

An hour later, I was still mooching around the house feeling sorry for myself and the walls were closing in on me. Enough was enough. To hell with this. To hell with Nathan. To hell with everything. I needed to get me some open space.

Donning my coat, I headed on out into a bright wet morning of blue skies and shimmering pavements. Bright droplets of rain hung on the underside of branches like glittering diamonds and the air was fresh and full of the sea. I breathed it all in, glad to be away from the oppressive confines of the house.

This wasn't weather for wasting. I hopped into the Elan and drove out to the coast road with the hood down, keeping the sea on my left, and raced along the town perimeter, taking the long route around to the vicarage.

Now Lowe had given the go-ahead, I would sort through the rest of my father's papers and, task completed, hand over the keys to Trivett and never have to see the place again. But first, I wanted to put my troubles behind me for a while and feel the wind in my face.

Aeons-old mineral deposits glinted in the crumbling face of the red crag cliffs to my right and rock pools, dotted along the scree-lined base, flashed reflected sunlight as I sped past. By the time I reached the far side of Tinkers Wood on the other side of town, my gloomy mood had lifted. At the turn into Vicarage Lane, my mobile rang, lifting my mood even more. Nathan? It had to be.

The moment I reached the vicarage courtyard, I pulled up to the gate under the sombre shade of the roadside elms, and checked the call.

It wasn't him. My heart sank again. Another disappointment.

Why was I fooling myself? If he was going to call, he would have done so by now.

The call was from Erin Corby. I couldn't imagine what she wanted to talk about. At our last meeting, I'd offered to help with counselling for Laura. But that was more of a courtesy than anything and I hadn't expected her to take me up on it.

As I crossed the rain-washed courtyard, I returned her call but there was no reply. I left a message.

I opened the vicarage door and, startled, took an involuntary step back and sucked in air. It was a disaster zone. I don't know what had made me think the police would clear up the mess. But why would they?

Clothing was strewn around the floor, papers and documents scattered everywhere.

I stepped out of the sunlight into the dark musty hall, pushed the door to behind me, and moved around cautiously, stopping now and then to move some clutter out of the way with my foot as I followed the trail of debris, checking out each room before making my way back to the hall.

Scenes of disarray were everywhere.

This had been more than a frenetic search for something. It had been an act of violence. Contents of cupboards and drawers hadn't just been tipped out onto the floor but flung around as if in anger. One of the desk drawers in the study had been yanked off its runners. In the dining room, the drapes framing the now boarded-up French doors had been ripped down and thrown to one side. The disarray extended to the kitchen where broken crockery covered the worktops.

I pictured myself back on the hall floor, unconscious and powerless, while someone raged around me, trashing the place. My body tingled. How vulnerable I must have been, lying there, out cold, at the mercy of that violent intruder.

What was so important that someone would risk such a desperate act? What was I missing?

Without any obvious pointers, it was futile to speculate. And so I pushed all such thoughts aside to focus instead on the job in hand. In these stale empty rooms, away from the warming power of the sun, the air was cold. The smell of decay hung around like bad breath. The sooner I completed my task, the sooner I could leave this sickly old house behind for good.

I cleared away most of the mess, gathered together all the

scattered papers and documents, and carried them through to the study. Seated at my father's desk, still wearing my coat to guard against the damp, I worked through the morning until I had reorganised all the documents into a number of piles according to their nature and importance. Task completed, I compiled an inventory.

Before leaving, I hunted around for Jonas Wainwright's toolbox and found it in the kitchen under a paint-stained dust sheet.

I took it with me, gathered up the documents on the way, and made my way out, taking a last look around the dismal rooms as I headed for the door.

Dust motes hung in the air, caught by hazy sunlight that found its way in through grimy windows. The heavy old furniture was worn and faded. All was silent. The grandfather clock that had stood guard by the outer door for so long, ticking away the years, was now mute. It was as if the place itself, bereft of human life, was dying.

Maybe, one day, a new incumbent would bring it back to life. But I was glad to be seeing it for the last time.

I locked the door behind me, put Jonas's toolbox in the boot of the Elan, and hurried over to Trivett's house with the keys and inventory.

Giles Trivett greeted me on the doorstep, fussing around me like an old mother hen, clucking and squawking his concerns about the recent break-in, wringing his hands, and expressing his hope that I was fully recovered.

"It's one terrible event after another. And to think that we were just a few yards away. I can't begin to tell you how distressed I was."

Anyone listening in, would have thought he'd been the one to suffer the ordeal.

I assured him I was fine, and I'd suffered no ill effects. "I'm just grateful to be in one piece." Making light of my experience, I tapped my head and said, "Being thickheaded has its advantages sometimes."

Seemingly reassured, he invited me in and apologised for his wife not being at home to wait on us. "She had some shopping to do," he explained.

Oh, yes? How many times had she used that as an excuse? "I'm not staying," I said. "I just wanted to drop off the keys. I won't be needing them anymore."

Along with the keys and inventory, I gave him a note of my mobile number and contact details in case he needed to get in touch with me.

"I hope you can read my handwriting," I said. "I tried using my father's old typewriter but I couldn't get to grips with it. It was like trying to drive a tank. I can't believe people still use those old things."

He laughed. "Your father was a bit of a Luddite in that respect. He hated modern technology; mobile phones, computers. He wouldn't even use a calculator. I'm surprised a typewriter wasn't too high-tech for him."

I pulled a face. "Yes, that sounds like my father."

Trivett said, "He used to say that our brains were a divine gift and anything that prevented us from using them was an insult to God." He tutted. "He could be quite dogmatic about such things."

My father could be dogmatic about most things but perhaps it wasn't the time to say so.

A light rain had blown in from the sea, and so, eager to get away, I wished him well and took my leave.

I hurried back to the car without a backward glance, leaving my old childhood home behind me forever.

CHAPTER THIRTY-SEVEN

I sank my teeth into a double decker smothered with melted cheese.

This place made the best burgers in town and I was ravenous. Skipping breakfast had made me even hungrier.

Karen said, "You look like you needed that."

I swallowed and said, "After the morning I've had, you bet I needed it. This is comfort food."

We were sharing a table by the window in the Grill Bar on the Esplanade. It was early afternoon and the staff were busy catering to the lunchtime crowd. From behind the counter, a pimply youth with a pencil moustache barked out table numbers for orders of burgers and fries. All around us, other diners chatted and laughed over their meals. It was a pleasant contrast to the gloomy silence of the vicarage.

I'd managed to persuade Karen to take a break and join me for lunch. After a few cheerless hours on my own, I was as much in need of company as food and was enjoying the change of atmosphere.

Karen cut into a baked potato stuffed with tuna mayo. "Bad day?"

"Just putting the past to rest."

"What?" she wrinkled her forehead.

In between mouthfuls, I filled her in on my day so far, starting with Lowe's visit and ending with handing the vicarage keys over to Trivett. "I was glad to get it over with. I feel I can put the past behind me now and move on."

Of course, the other reason for my doleful disposition was Nathan's lack of communication. But I didn't want to get into that. It would depress me again, and I was trying to stay upbeat.

"Well, that's one problem out of the way." She took a mouthful of food and chewed it thoughtfully. Finally, "Nothing else on your mind?"

Halfway through raising a forkful of coleslaw to my mouth, I paused. Something in her tone suggested it was more than a casual question. "Should there be?"

"Just wondered," she said, keeping her attention fixed on her plate.

"There's nothing in particular," I said, guardedly. "Why do you ask?"

"No reason." She kept her eyes down.

Lowering my fork, I said. "Come on, out with it."

"What?" She looked up, all innocence.

I put down my cutlery, folded my arms, and stared at her through narrowed eyes. "Listen, lady, I know when you're skirting around something. So let's have it."

There was a defiant gleam in her eyes. "I had coffee with Nathan earlier."

For a moment, I said nothing and then pushed the plated remains of my meal to one side, no longer hungry. "Great."

That came out louder than I'd intended.

A young woman in Grill Bar livery, cleaning the next table, broke off from her task and beamed over to me. "I'm so glad you're enjoying it, Sir. Please feel free to take part in our online customer survey if you have the time. The details are on the menu."

I smiled wanly, assured her I would be happy to do so, and turned back to Karen. Lowering my voice, I leaned forward and said, "So he found time to talk to you this morning but he's too busy to get in touch with me."

"So there is something wrong then?"

"You tell me. You're the one he talks to." I leaned back, picked up my beaker of now lukewarm coffee and took a long swig. I was peeved. "What did he say? Is he giving me the run around?"

"Have you two been arguing?"

"Far from it."

"What do you mean?"

"Nothing." Bad slip. Talking over the more intimate aspects of my relationship with Nathan had been the last thing on my mind. And it was a dead cert he wouldn't have said anything.

The Slow Road to Hell

Ever the soul of discretion.

The guy behind the counter called out more orders. Nearby a piece of cutlery clattered to the floor and someone laughed.

"Mikey!"

I winced. There seemed little point holding back. She would nag me till I told her. I glanced around to make sure no one was within earshot and, lowering my voice, said, "He stayed over."

"He stayed ..?" She paused. And then the blank stare changed to one of enlightenment. "Ah. So that's it."

"That's what?"

"Why he was in such a crabby mood this morning."

"Oh, thank you. That says a lot for your opinion of my sexual allure."

"He just doesn't know where he stands with you."

"What the hell did he think last night was about?"

"He probably thought it was a one-off. A parting shot."

"Oh, please."

"Come on, Mikey. Let's face it, when it comes to commitment, you've not had a great track record over the years."

I couldn't argue with that so I said nothing. I pulled my plate back toward me and stabbed at a gherkin. We both focused on our meals for a while.

Karen finished her meal and put down her fork. "You're sending out mixed messages. No wonder his head's all over the place." She picked up her coke and sipped it. "He's asked you several times what your plans are and you just brush him off."

"I have no idea what my plans are 'cos I don't have any."

Karen leaned toward me and said, "What is it you want, Mikey?"

A young couple brushed past us on their way to the door, calling out farewells to friends at another table. We sat without speaking until they had passed by.

I said, "I want him back. There, I'd said it. Plain and simple."

"So why are you telling me and not him?"

Why did she need to ask? It should have been obvious. "How can I? What am I supposed to say? Sorry, I was wrong? Let's just pick up where we left off?" I stared down at my plate and shoved some salad around with my fork. "I don't have the right. I know how much I hurt him. God knows, he made that clear enough."

Karen reached over and pressed a hand on top of mine. "And that's why you have to make the first move, tell him how you feel. Because he's not going to. It's a case of once bitten, twice shy. If you're serious about getting him back, you're going to have to make the running. You're the one who has to put it right."

CHAPTER THIRTY-EIGHT

Karen was right of course. She usually was. It was one of her more annoying qualities.

And it looked as if I would be able to put her advice into effect sooner than I thought; Nathan's Astra was parked on the doorstep when I reached home.

I slammed the door of the Elan and hurried over to him as he climbed out of his car. "Where the hell have you been? I've been trying to get hold of you all day."

He frowned and fixed me with a glassy stare. "I do have a job to do, Mikey."

That stopped me short. Was that it? No apology? I'd been waiting all this time to find out why he'd sneaked off in the early hours, why the hell he hadn't been in touch, and all I got was this short rebuttal. Who the fuck did he think I was. I was pissed.

"I hope this is important then. God forbid I should take up any of your valuable time."

"Erin Corby's been murdered, and you were the last person she spoke to. Is that important enough?"

There was a rushing sound in my head and I froze where I stood as his words sank in, my mind in turmoil. And then I stepped back, open-mouthed. Not sure what to say.

An old Mark II Cortina passed by and tooted to a young woman pushing a pram on the other side of the road. She waved back. Further down the road, someone opened a window and called out to an elderly man clipping his garden hedge. Sunlight, momentarily caught in the moving glass, flashed and caught my eye.

A light breeze stirred some fallen leaves at our feet.

This was a sleepy backwater town. Nothing special. Just ordinary folk going about their ordinary mundane lives. And Erin Corby was one of them. An ordinary pleasant woman with a cheerful disposition getting on with her life. This wasn't supposed to happen to people like her. Nothing bad was supposed to happen here.

My stomach knotted. It was all too much. When I spoke, the words came out in a strained croak. "How? When?"

The blood drained from my face and my legs gave beneath me. I reached out to steady myself against the side of Nathan's Astra. The metal was cold beneath my hand.

He reached out and took me by the arm. When he spoke again, his tone was softer. "Hey, come on. Let's get you inside."

With a shaking hand, I fumbled for my keys. He took them from me, opened the door, and ushered me inside.

Not bothering to remove my coat, I made straight for the couch and dropped onto it. My heart raced. "What happened?"

Nathan headed for the kitchen sink. He returned with a tumbler of water and handed it to me. "Here, I think you need this."

I needed a damn sight more than a glass of water but I took it anyway. My throat was dry, and I gulped down half of it in one go.

He seated himself in the facing chair and said, "It was a hit and run."

I drained what was left of the water. "It was an accident then?"

"Circumstances suggest otherwise."

My heart jumped a beat. "What circumstances?"

"We'll leave that aside for the moment. Right now I need to establish the events that led up to her death. That's why I'm here."

Nathan had adopted his formal tone, and I was apprehensive. My hand tightened on the empty tumbler. I put it aside on the coffee table next to me. "What does it have to do with me?"

"I checked her mobile. She called you just before it happened. And you returned her call." He unbuttoned his coat and settled back in his chair. "What was that about?"

"I have no idea."

"What's that supposed to mean?"

"Exactly that. I missed her call when I was on the road. I tried to get back to her, but she didn't pick up." She may well have been killed between the time she called me and the time I called her back. I shuddered. It wasn't something I wanted to dwell on.

"You must have some idea."

Nathan hadn't fully turned off the kitchen tap and there was a constant drip drip drip of water into the sink. For some irrational reason, it annoyed me.

I snapped, "If I knew, I'd tell you. I have no idea what she wanted. I was surprised to get the call."

Nathan narrowed his eyes. "You've not been interfering again, taking things into your own hands? 'Cos I warn you, if you have ..."

"No, I damn well haven't." Why did he always have to think the worst of me?

He grunted, as if doubting me. But he didn't pursue it. "What about that problem with the bracelet? How did that go?"

"Erin gave it back to me. And promised to talk to Laura and keep an eye on her. Problem solved."

"There has to be some reason for her call."

"I'm sure there does. But I don't know what it is." He kept pushing me as if I would suddenly come up with an answer. I was getting more agitated by the minute. "Sorry but I can't help."

I pushed myself up out of my seat and went and turned off the dripping tap. "Where did it happen?"

"Tinkers Wood. She was on her way back from Wainwright's place. So I guess she must have called you from there."

Reaching up to the cupboard above the sink, I took out a whiskey glass. I was in dire need of a strong pick-me-up. "What makes you so sure it wasn't an accident?"

I went to the drinks cabinet and unscrewed a bottle of Glenfiddick Malt. Nathan shot me a disapproving look, but I ignored it.

"We have a witness." he said. "A local woman. She was walking her dog on the edge of the wood and saw the whole thing."

Halfway through filling my glass, I stopped. "How can she be sure it wasn't an accident?"

Nathan swallowed hard. "Erin was running from the car. It

mounted the pavement and ran her down."

"Oh my God." I poured another shot of whiskey into my glass and took a large swig. "Did this witness see who did it?"

"She was too far away. And the car made a U turn and headed off in the other direction."

I made my way back to my seat. The bright chime of the Westminster clock on the mantelpiece interrupted the silence as I dropped into my chair.

I struggled to make sense of the various events of the past few days. "There has to be some connection to the other two murders. It can't just be coincidence. That would be too much to take on board." I swallowed another large mouthful of whiskey.

Nathan squirmed in his chair. "On the face of it, there's nothing to tie Erin's death to those of your father and Black. But there is one common element." He tugged at his shirt collar. "They all seem to point to you."

"Me?" I tensed and almost spilled my whiskey. I put the glass down on the coffee table next to the tumbler. "What are you saying?"

He spread his hands and said, "Look, Mikey, your father was the first victim. Then you're attacked in the vicarage. And now Erin is killed after trying to contact you. There has to be some connection."

Protesting, I said, "I don't see that. This is a small town. Everyone knows everyone. And Erin knew both my father and Black. She worked for them." I was trying to convince myself as much as him. Any connection to a triple murder, however tenuous, was too close for comfort.

"That may well be," he said, "but calling you just before she was killed seems more than just coincidence. You need to have a good hard think about that call. See if you can come up with anything. It could well point us to whoever did this."

It was a second or so before I realised I was gripping the arms of my chair. I relaxed my hands. "What frame of mind was she in before it happened? Did Wainwright notice anything?"

"He was at work. She has her own key."

"So she was there alone?"

"It would seem so." He buttoned up his coat and said, "I'm going to have to get back, Mikey. There's a lot to do." He rose to leave. "But please let me know if you think of anything that might help. Even the smallest detail may be useful."

"Of course I will" I rose too and walked him to the door.

He still hadn't explained his early departure that morning. Or why he hadn't returned any of my calls. The shock at learning of Erin's death had put it out of my mind. But now I remembered. And I was puzzled. Tentatively, I asked, "Will I see you later?"

He swallowed and said, "I'm going to be tied up for most of the day. Sorry. I do have a lot on."

"Tonight?"

"I need to get back to Charwell tonight. I don't have a change of clothes over here and I'm still wearing yesterday's."

Why did I get the impression I was being given the brush off? I tried again. "You could bring some back with you and stay over."

"Look, Mikey, it's best if I don't." His tone was almost pleading. "Right now I need to stay focused. No distractions."

A heaviness settled on me and there was a sour taste in my mouth. "Is that what I am? A distraction?"

"That's not what I meant."

"I'm confused. I feel like I've done something wrong and I don't know what. After last night, I thought we were friends again."

"Friends? I don't want ..." He cut himself short. The muscles in his jaw tightened. Always a sure sign he was annoyed or upset about something. I wished I knew what.

I said, "Please talk to me, Nathan. I want to know where I stand."

He rocked back on his heels and then tilted his head to one side and fixed me with a quizzical look as if weighing up his words. Finally, he said, "Okay. Time for some straight talking."

"I just want you to be honest with me. I get the feeling you've been avoiding me."

"After last night, I needed some time alone. That's why I didn't call you. I had some thinking to do."

"What was there to think about?"

"I asked you last night if it was a game changer. Remember? You brushed it aside like it wasn't important. Well, you need to know that to me it was important. Last night was important. I felt let down. I don't think it meant as much to you as it did to me."

That was a shock. Right out of left field. How had I missed it? "Is that why you left without waking me?"

He didn't reply. Just stared back at me with a pained look on his face as if unable to understand how I could be so slow on the uptake.

I said, "You're wrong. If that's what you thought, you're wrong. I wanted to enjoy the moment without thinking about anything else. That's all. I was content, happy to be where I was. Right then nothing else mattered."

"Well maybe it should have mattered. And I've asked you several times what your plans are. Each time you just put me off."

"What are you saying? That last night was a mistake?"

"I'm saying that last night made me think long and hard about where this was going."

"And where did all this thinking lead you?"

"You asked me to be honest with you, so I will be. You let me down once before. Badly. And it took me a long time to get over it."

He paused again, and I sensed some unpleasant home truth was on the way.

He continued. "I'm not sure I can trust you, Mikey. And I don't want to go through all that again."

Trust? That was the issue? He didn't trust me?

I was stunned.

We'd spent a night of shared intimacy together, as close as two people can ever be, and he was telling me he didn't trust me.

Resentment welled up inside me. "If you think so little of me, why did you bother to stay over?"

"You're not being fair, Mikey. That's not what I think. I'm just not sure you know what you want right now. And I think it best if I took a step back."

My throat tightened and when I spoke, my voice was strained. "I guess there's nothing more to say then, is there?"

He was wrong. I did know what I wanted. But there seemed little point in telling him. No matter how much he tried to wrap it up in weasel words, his intention was clear enough. I didn't need it spelling out. He was giving me the push.

CHAPTER THIRTY-NINE

Deadlines. I hated them. On the positive side, they usually focused my attention remarkably well on the task in hand. Usually. But not today.

I was fast approaching my publisher's deadline for a treatise on the abnormal psychology of serial killers, and I needed to buckle down to some serious in-depth research. Not the most lighthearted of subjects but it matched my mood.

Right then, however, despite my best intentions, I found it difficult to concentrate on the warped mentalities of our more nefarious members of society. Nathan's not-quite-as-warped mentality was of more concern.

Two days later, I was still brooding over our heart-to-heart. I sat at the kitchen table, a laptop in front of me surrounded by piles of books and papers, and stared into space, chewing the end of my pen while I chewed over his words.

Had I got it wrong? Was he looking for a way to end our relationship before it started? Or was he being true to his word? Taking it slow? I vacillated between the two possibilities, confident and upbeat one moment, convinced that we would work through our differences, and depressed and downbeat the next, sure that he was determined to put a stop to any possible relationship. If only I could make up my mind one way or the other. Then at least I would be able to come to terms with the situation and decide how to handle it. And, perhaps, be able to concentrate on my work.

Ted Bundy, one of America's more notorious serial killers, stared up at me from the cover of the book I was holding, a cheerful grin on his face. I glowered back at him and shoved the book to one side, reluctant to delve into it. I poured myself a glass of wine instead. This was one deadline I was going to miss.

It was during one of my many breaks, frustrated at not being able to focus, that I learned of Adam Corby's arrest for his wife's murder.

I hadn't heard from Nathan since his fond farewell speech - if that's what it was - so I was out of touch with what was happening on the front line of Elders Edge police force. It was Lowe who told me.

I was over at the Fairview having coffee with Karen and trying to fend off questions about my meeting with Nathan. Lowe had dropped round on his way to the station to apologise for yet another missed date. While Karen sat and sulked over her coffee, I pumped Lowe for more information.

"So it was his car that ran her down?" I said.

"We found it abandoned on some waste ground on the other side of Tinkers Wood."

"But you say he'd reported it stolen?"

"Yeah, right. How very convenient."

Karen interjected. "She was such a nice woman. What a terrible thing to happen." She pushed her empty mug away from her and rose from the table around which we'd all been seated. "I'll get another jug of coffee," she said, and left the room.

While she was away, Lowe went into more detail about Corby's arrest, and explained how the car had been found during a routine patrol not long after it had been called in stolen.

He said, "The car was damaged. A smashed front wing. And it was covered in blood. Forensics are all over it at the moment but I have no doubt they'll link it to Erin Corby's death."

"What makes you so sure Corby was at the wheel?"

"His alibi didn't stand up. And now - surprise, surprise - he can't remember where he was."

Before I could push him for more details, Karen returned with the coffee and Lowe said to her, "I didn't know you knew Erin."

Karen seated herself, poured herself a coffee, and passed the jug over to Lowe. "I didn't. I just met her the once when she came to see Mikey. But I had a long chat with her. I liked her."

Lowe filled his mug and put the jug on the table. "You have to wonder why he would want to kill her," he said. "But then there's no knowing what goes on behind other people's closed doors."

Maybe he should be doing more than just wondering. He should be investigating what went on behind those closed doors and, at the very least, look for a plausible motive.

"I have to say, I didn't take to him," Karen said. "I got the impression he neglected her, off out with his friends all the time. She seemed to spend all her time working, hadn't been out socially for weeks."

I turned my attention to Lowe and said, "What was his alibi?"

"First, he said he was at home alone. But he'd already told us he was out when his car was stolen. So that didn't stand up. Then he decided he was shopping in town. Trouble is, he can't remember what shops he went in and neither can any of the shopkeepers. And now the guy's changing his story every five minutes."

For Lowe at least, it was cut and dried. No point exploring other options when a simple link presented itself. Corby owned the car that killed his wife. Ergo, Corby killed his wife.

But something wasn't right. Abandoning the car and then reporting it stolen might make sense but the lack of an alibi was a different matter. If Corby had killed his wife, it would have to be premeditated, and only a fool would kill in such circumstances and not try to fabricate, in advance, a plausible account of his whereabouts. And Adam Corby hadn't struck me as being a fool. He wouldn't be left floundering like this if he had killed Erin.

No, it didn't ring true. There had to be another explanation for his lack of a valid alibi. And only one explanation came to mind. One that would put him in the clear.

Lowe finished his coffee and left for the station. I left soon after to avoid Karen interrogating me any more about my meeting with Nathan.

Back home, I tried to get stuck into my research but I still couldn't concentrate. My attention was elsewhere. Not so much on Nathan this time. I couldn't stop thinking about the circumstances surrounding Erin's death. I didn't buy Lowe's interpretation of events.

Eventually, I called Lowe at the station.

"I've been going over what you told me about Corby," I said. "I think it's time we got on with those interviews."

"Yes, of course," he said. "But there's no connection between this investigation and your father's murder."

"I wouldn't be so sure, " I said. "And anyway, it's not him I'm interested in right now. I want you to re-interview Frances Trivett as a priority."

CHAPTER FORTY

We were back in Lowe's office. Nathan, Lowe and I. Lowe was leaning over the desk fiddling with the brightness control on the monitor. The image on the screen was of the interview room next door. Just three chairs were visible. The table had been removed at my request.

"Thanks for this, Nathan," I said.

It was only yesterday I'd asked Lowe to make Frances Trivett's interview a priority and Nathan had been quick to act in setting it up.

He smiled. An easy relaxed smile. "It's not a problem," he said. "We were going to re-interview her anyway."

Any apprehension I'd felt about seeing him again after the way our last encounter ended had been quickly dispelled. I'd been worried that he'd meant to put the dampers on our relationship and would try to distance himself. But he was surprisingly affable.

He continued, "I'm not sure what you'll get out of it though."

"We'll see."

I'd already explained the procedure I generally followed for such interviews. For me, it was just another well-worn routine. One I'd gone through many times before.

First, I observed the interviewee's reactions under questioning and noted any discrepancies between body language and verbal communication, any individual tics or tells that conflicted with their verbal responses.

Once I'd assessed the veracity or otherwise of their disclosures and noted any possible weaknesses, I would introduce myself in my professional capacity and establish my credentials.

Faced with the professional judgement of someone they accepted as an expert in the field, most subjects would give way when confronted by any evidence of deceit.

And that was the next stage. Confrontation. Applying pressure specifically in those areas already flagged as potential trouble spots.

Sometimes, it all went to plan. Other times, it took more effort. But I usually got there in the end.

I asked, "Who's carrying out the interview?"

Lowe answered. "Miles Barber." He finished fiddling with the monitor and leaned back in his chair. "He's good. An experienced interviewer. And he's already been briefed on what to ask."

At that moment, the monitor screen showed Constable Barber usher Frances Trivett into the interview room and while they took their seats and made themselves comfortable, Lowe showed me how to use the microphone. "Press this switch here if you need a particular question asked" he said, pointing to the base of the microphone stand. "Barber is wearing an earpiece so he'll pick up any instructions we pass on to him."

"Okay," I said.

We sat together around the table and watched the screen.

I wasn't having an easy time of this. Being around Nathan. I'd kept my feelings hidden for so long - even from myself - and now I'd finally come to terms with how I felt about him, it was a strain keeping up the just-good-buddies routine.

He was friendly enough. I wasn't getting the cold treatment anymore. Or the seething anger. But that was part of the problem. Whenever he smiled at me with that big wide grin that made the left side of his cheek dimple, there was a tightness in my throat and I had to force myself to relax and smile back in that casual way that friends do.

There had been a time, whenever we sat together like this, side by side, he would occasionally squeeze my thigh to emphasise a point he was making or slow punch my arm or wrap an arm around my waist. It was these small intimate gestures I missed. Those shared moments between lovers that I had taken for granted.

How did he really feel? Was this as much a charade for him as it was for me? Or was he content to be just friends?

I turned my attention to the screen. All thoughts of Nathan and my own problems would have to wait. This was going to need my full concentration.

Frances Trivett was speaking. "Do I have to go through it all again?"

"Nothing to worry about," said Barber. "In light of new developments, we're re-interviewing everyone who knew either the Reverend MacGregor or Dr Black. I understand Black was your doctor?"

"Yes," Frances said. "And, of course, we knew him socially too."

"So you would have no trouble recognising his voice?"

"That's right. He has a very distinctive voice."

"And there's no doubt that the voice you heard on ..." He paused, looked down at his notes and ran his finger down the page before looking up again. "... on the 3rd of February, was that of Derek Black?"

Frances Trivett shuffled in her seat and crossed her legs, locking her ankles together. "None at all," she said, raising a hand to her throat.

I leaned closer to the screen. "Look," I said, "you see what she did with her feet? That's why I wanted the desk removed. We could have missed that otherwise. And the hand. You see what she did?"

"I see it," Nathan said, "but I don't know what it signifies, if anything."

I said, "What you just saw was an innate response of the body's limbic system, the part of our brain that deals with autonomic reflexes."

Nathan affirmed his understanding.

Lowe looked confused. His own body language told me much about his inability to deal with novel ideas. But perhaps it wasn't the best of times to tell him so.

Keeping part of my attention on the continuing interview, I said, "Look, whenever we're faced with a threatening situation, our bodies respond automatically."

Nathan said, "The fight-or-flight response?"

"Yes. It's one of two knee-jerk reactions we make when faced with danger."

"I've heard of that," said Lowe.

I continued. "Well, it's the wrong way around and it's incomplete. Our bodies respond to danger in one of three ways, and each of them is attempted in strict sequence. Freeze, flight or fight, in that order."

"And how does that relate to what we just saw?" Nathan asked.

Lowe grunted. He didn't sound convinced.

This was another part of my well-worn routine. Having to explain and justify my particular field of study to an uncomprehending and unbelieving audience. To someone like Lowe, and to many others in the force I'd had to deal with, it was mumbo-jumbo, and I constantly had to prove myself, satisfy others that I wasn't a charlatan.

I said, "She's displaying a consistent pattern of behaviours I would expect to find when someone is lying. For example, did you see the way she kept looking towards the door? That's the second response, flight."

Lowe laughed and said, "She's hardly going to make a run for it."

"Of course not. But what keeps her in place is her conscious awareness of the situation she's in. But at the subconscious level, she's looking for a means of escape. And so her body responds automatically."

"Fascinating stuff," said Nathan.

"Yes," said Lowe, not sounding in the least bit fascinated.

I said, "I'm not suggesting it's easy to interpret. You need to take account of the subject's baseline behaviour and look for specific responses that deviate from the baseline."

"That's all very well," said Nathan, "but we're going to need more than your interpretation of her body language. So far, we haven't found cause to disprove her version of events."

"Well, let's see what we can do, shall we?" Rising to my feet, I said, "Let Constable Barber know I'm on my way in, will you? I've seen all I need to see."

A moment later, I was in the interview room, reintroducing

myself to Frances. I drew up a chair next to Miles Barber and sat down.

She looked surprised. "I hadn't realised you were taking part in the investigation." She appeared resentful. A far cry from her behaviour at our first meeting.

"It's what I do for a living, Frances. I put together psychological profiles of suspects and witnesses on behalf of the police. Part of my work involves matching interviews against behaviour patterns as a way to assess if a witness is telling the truth or not." So she would be in no doubt about my authority, I added, "I've worked for many forces over the years with excellent results. I'm very good at what I do."

She reacted much as I had anticipated. Her chair creaked as she shifted position and raised a hand to her throat, playing with the gold chain necklace around her neck. A typical pacifying action. And then she crossed her arms in a defensive move.

I increased the pressure. "I've been looking through your witness statement and I have to say, it makes interesting reading. Especially, in light of the reactions I've observed in this present interview." Pointing up to the camera in the corner of the room, I continued. "I've been watching your behaviour on the monitor next door."

She gripped the chain, twisting it tight, and wrapped her feet around the legs of her chair. A freeze response. She showed all the signs of being trapped.

So far, so good. Time to move in for the kill. I'd seen enough to know she was lying and, just as importantly, why.

"I know how frustrating this must be, Frances. But I'm sure you must want to help as much as possible. You want us to catch this murderer, right?"

"Of course I do." She sounded indignant.

"And you've heard about Adam Corby's arrest?"

"Yes." She avoided my eyes.

"Erin was a friend of yours, wasn't she? It must be very painful for you knowing her husband has been charged with her murder."

"He didn't kill her."

"You seem very certain of that."

She squirmed uneasily. "He had no reason to. He's a kind docile man."

"Maybe. But as long as he continues to lie about his whereabouts, no one is going to believe that."

She was silent again.

I said, "I suppose you must think that the truth will out eventually. And that Adam will be released."

"Yes, I do." Her tone was defiant.

"I'm afraid that's not how it works, Frances. There are just three possible outcomes here. Either Adam continues to lie and is prosecuted for Erin's murder. Or the truth will be uncovered and your relationship with Adam will be made public, exposing you to a great deal of embarrassment, and, of course, you'll be charged with wasting police time in respect of both Erin's murder and my father's. The third choice is for you to tell the truth now and save yourself from public exposure and from facing criminal charges. So which is it to be, Frances?"

As I spoke, the look of stubborn defiance faded and her face crumpled. Her subterfuge had been exposed for what it was and she must have known she had no choice but to come clean. Close to tears, she managed to keep control of herself and, with bowed head, accepted the inevitable.

"So where was Adam when Erin was killed?"

"There's a place we go to. The Sea Spray boarding house on the Charwell Road. Adam books a room there."

"And you were there when Erin was killed?"

She sniffled and nodded.

Did Adam Corby drive there?"

"No. He was always worried about the car being spotted. He left the car at home and used the bus." Her voice was breaking up.

"And when Jonas heard my father arguing with Black? You were with Adam then, weren't you? You never heard that argument."

"No." She pulled a tissue from the sleeve of her blouse and blew her nose. "I panicked. Giles couldn't understand why I didn't recognise his voice. We know him so well. So I went along with it. Said I was there."

I said, "Best if we take another statement from you, Frances. And let's have it like it really was this time."

"Yes," she said.

CHAPTER FORTY-ONE

I loved my early morning runs. That rush of adrenaline pumping through my muscles, the steady rhythm of my body as it pushed against its limits, the cold air against my face. It was a time to think, to work through my problems and plan my day. This morning was no different; so many things to think about.

The pavement, slick and wet from the overnight rain, glistened and gleamed in the early morning light as I sprinted along the sea front. A pale amber sun rose from the sea, spreading its golden glow across the water.

There were few people around so early; three or four other runners on the Esplanade and a small number of shopkeepers opening up for the day. Jack Warrinder, proprietor of Warrinder's Emporium was setting out his wares in front of the shop and waved as I passed by. I can still remember when he bought the shop as a young man after his marriage to a local beauty. Now he was well into middle-age with a paunch and a balding pate. A few suited commuters trekked by on their way to the railway station to begin another day in London city offices.

I was on a high, invigorated, ready to tackle anything.

Yesterday's breakthrough with Frances Trivett had confirmed what I had always suspected about her relationship with Adam Corby, vindicating my suspicions, and, although it hadn't moved the investigation forward, it had at least put it back on the right track.

Nathan hadn't been in a mood to let them off lightly, despite my telling Frances otherwise. He intended to throw the book at them. They would both face charges for wasting police time and suffer the humiliation of exposure.

For my part, I was more upbeat than I had been for the past few days. Nathan had been pleased with the way the interview had concluded. And was being friendly again. He'd promised to call me for a get together once the immediate pressure of work had eased off. And now I was in a better frame of mind, I saw our relationship for what it was.

I understood why Nathan was reluctant to trust me again. Karen was right. Once bitten, twice shy. But I was sure his feelings hadn't changed. It was me who had been the problem. And if I could show him that he could depend on me, that I was around for the long haul, I knew our relationship could flourish again.

God knows I could be difficult at times. And our past relationship hadn't always been an easy one. But I was certain that, deep down, his feelings were as strong as ever. Now that I'd realised how much I needed him, I had no intention of giving up on him. I was going to get him back, no matter what. And with that decision made, I was confident of a more certain future, sure of where I was going.

By the time I reached home, I was in a more positive frame of mind and even the presence of a reporter on my doorstep didn't change my mood.

He saw me approach and walked toward me, smiling, hand outstretched. A good-looking guy, about my age, short brown hair in a Caesar-style buzz cut, electric blue eyes in a clean-shaven tanned face and an open guileless expression. The clean-cut country-boy look was completed by a pair of faded denim jeans, a navy deck jacket, and a blue-stripe beach scarf wrapped twice around his neck.

"Michael MacGregor?" He said.

I'd done my best to keep my hideaway secret, watching out for any of the media guys and making sure I wasn't followed. But I suppose it was inevitable that they would find me eventually. Not that it would get them anywhere.

I ignored the hand. "You're wasting your time. I'm not giving interviews."

The smile faded. And then he beamed again and burst into laughter. "Just as well I'm not asking for one then." He offered his hand again. "The name's Brandon Barwell."

It took a moment for it to sink in and when it did, I clasped his hand and shook it firmly. "I'm so sorry. That was so presumptuous of me. You're the last person I expected to see."

He laughed again and said, "Not a problem. I hope it's okay me dropping by like this. There were some personal papers I needed to pick up."

"Of course I don't mind. It's your house after all."

"I wasn't sure if you'd mind or not. Nathan said it might not be a good idea."

"You've spoken to him today?" I dug the house keys out of my pocket and turned away to unlock the door.

"I'm staying with him over at Charwell."

I stiffened. Trying to keep the tension out of my voice, I said, "He never mentioned it." I was glad he couldn't see the expression on my face at that moment. My hand trembled as I turned the key to let us in.

"I got here the other day," he said, and followed me inside.

I headed for the kitchen table and sat down heavily. Nathan hadn't so much as hinted at Brandon Barwell's visit and to find out like this, having it come out of the blue without warning, hit me hard. I was shaken. Given the nature of their relationship, I was in no doubt that this was more than a casual visit.

"My stuff's upstairs," Brandon said. He was still smiling. "Just some invoices and receipts I need for my tax returns."

"Please," I said, waving a hand towards the stairs, "don't let me stop you."

"I'll go get them," he said and bounded upstairs, taking the steps two at a time. He called back down to me, "Nathan never told me he knew the famous Michael MacGregor."

I raised my voice so he would hear me. "I wouldn't call myself exactly famous."

As he rummaged around overhead, I tried to pull myself together, taking in some slow deep breaths to loosen the tightness in my chest.

Myriad questions rose in my mind and I struggled to form some answers to them. How had I not suspected something? Brandon must have arrived after Nathan and I spent the night together. Is that why Nathan had cooled toward me? Because Brandon was back? Is that why he had chosen not to stay over again? And why he had used pressure of work as an excuse to avoid me?

It now made sense. The signs had been there all along. But I'd been stupid enough to ignore them, preferring to believe instead that Nathan and I were becoming close again.

As these thoughts tumbled around in my head, Brandon reappeared with a sheaf of papers and a book in his hand. He jumped down the last couple of steps, dropped into one of the armchairs by the fireside, and unwound his scarf. Obviously not in a hurry to leave.

He grinned up at me and said, "Nathan knows how much I like your show. And he never said a word. Can you believe it?" He didn't stop for an answer. "You grew up together didn't you?"

He was animated, energetic, full of enthusiasm. We were of similar ages and yet he made me feel old and jaded. When had I stopped being all the things he was now? Was it when all those early dreams and hopes had faded to nothing? When I'd stopped caring and settled for less? No wonder Nathan had taken to him. It would be hard not to be captivated.

I forced a smile. "It was a lifetime ago. We haven't been in touch for ages."

A hollowness opened and spread inside me and what small burgeoning hope I'd had of the future I'd planned for myself shrivelled and died. I twisted around and grabbed the towel I'd left hanging over the back of the chair and used it as an excuse to hide my face while I wiped away the sweat. I didn't want him to see how hurt I was. All that I'd hoped for had come to nothing. I'd been such a fool.

"I guess people drift apart," Brandon said. "Still it's good to catch up with old friends. It's just a shame you had to meet again in such circumstances."

I nodded and dropped the towel onto an adjacent chair, struggling to keep my feelings from showing. But he seemed oblivious to my mood. He was still talking ten to the dozen.

"Look," he said, "I hope you don't mind me asking but I have your book here about reading body language." He rose from his chair and came over to the table, holding it out to me. "Would you mind signing it for me? I'd really appreciate it." He seated himself at the table.

How could I refuse. I picked up my pen from among the papers scattered about the table, took the book from him and opened it at the flyleaf.

I said, "Nathan says you've known each other for a few years." Writing slowly to stop my hand from shaking, I signed the book and handed it back to him.

He took it from me and said, "Getting on for three years now. We met when I came down to finalise the purchase of this place. I was staying at the Fairview. The proprietor introduced us. Karen Dyer?" He laughed. "But of course you must know her if she's a friend of Nathan's."

"Karen's one of my closest friends," I said.

"I really like her," he said, enthusiastically. "I'm sure I'll get to know her better if things work out with Nathan."

"Work out?" The emptiness inside deepened and widened.

Oh, I'm sorry." He frowned. "You do know we're involved?"

"Yes, I had heard."

"I wasn't sure if you knew he was ... you know ... that we were ..."

"Yes, I did know. But I hadn't realised how close you were."

He grinned. "It's been a bit of a long-distance relationship so far. It's not easy when you live so far apart." The smile faded as he said this but he soon brightened again. "I think we've known each other long enough now. It's time we moved our relationship to the next level."

"So what are your plans?" I was finding it hard to keep the tremor from my voice.

"Obviously, Nathan's work will keep him down here. But there's no reason why I can't move." He explained, "I'm a freelance graphic designer so I can work from anywhere."

"How very convenient," I said.

He bounced in his chair and said, "And, of course, I want to get to know all Nathan's friends." He sounded hopeful. "I can't quite believe that Michael MacGregor stayed in my house."

That was the moment I made my decision. I had a vision of the future. Of Nathan and Brandon setting up home together. Laughing together. Making love. Sharing all those small intimacies that lovers do. The way Nathan and I once did.

There was no place for me here any more. It was strange how everything could change in an instant. Maybe one day Nathan would read the book I'd just signed and recognise my name. And maybe he would remember that we had once shared something special and muse on what might have been. But such a future wasn't to be and this is where the self-deception ended.

I said, "Well, I'm happy to say you can now have your house back."

"You're leaving?" His eyes widened. "Nathan said you'd be staying a while longer."

"No, I'm leaving."

He said, "Nathan's spending a lot of time down here at the moment. So I suppose it would be more convenient for us to stay here. But please don't let me drive you away. I'm happy to stay where I am for the moment if you still need the place."

"That's kind of you, thanks. But I need to get back to London."

"If you're sure."

"As a matter of fact, I'll need to start packing shortly. I'll be leaving tomorrow." I stood up, hoping he'd take the hint.

He took the hint, pushed back his chair and rose to his feet. "I'll leave you to it. I'm sure you have plenty to do."

"Oh, just one thing," he said. "Nathan asked me not to worry you. Said you didn't want to be disturbed. I was sure you wouldn't mind but Nathan can be a bit tetchy at times so if you'd mind not telling him I dropped by." Now he was embarrassed.

I offered him a reassuring smile. "I know what he can be like. Don't worry, I won't say a word. And I'll let him know I'm leaving."

He thanked me and I saw him out. He headed off with a confident jaunty walk.

On a small plot of land across the road, some bulbs were showing signs of early life, small green shoots struggling towards the light, signalling the coming spring, a time of renewal and fresh hope. And for some, new beginnings.

CHAPTER FORTY-TWO

Karen was having a hard time taking it in. "I don't get it. I spoke to him earlier And he never said a word."

I'd just told her about Nathan's visitor. Once I'd made the decision to return to London, I'd called to let her know about my abrupt change of plans.

I said. "What did you expect? After the other night?" He's not likely to broadcast it, is he?" I wasn't looking for reasons to defend him.

"Are you sure about this? You could be reading it all wrong. I thought you and he might ... you know .. I thought he was trying to patch things up."

"'Fraid not." I related the details of my conversation with Brandon that morning, and told her of my earlier one with Nathan, and even she, ever optimistic, had to concede defeat.

"I'm so sorry, Mikey. I don't know what to say."

"Not a lot you can say. I guess I have to accept the inevitable."

"Does Nathan know you're leaving?"

"Not yet. I'm driving back first thing in the morning. I'd rather leave it till the last minute before I tell him."

"If you're staying over, why don't you come round this evening for a drink? It would be nice to see you before you go and we can talk it through some more."

I wasn't sure what talking about it some more would achieve but at least I would have some much-needed company so I agreed.

"You can use the front entrance," Karen said. "I've closed the bar and restaurant for the evening so the press will have to find somewhere else to drink. Most of them have gone anyway. So we shouldn't be disturbed."

"I won't risk it," I said. "Those media guys are a sneaky lot."

The rest of the day passed in something of a haze. I made several phone calls, set up appointments for when I got back to London, and briefed my agent Jerry on my plans, going through the motions in a state of emotional numbness. I was determined to focus on the practicalities of getting my life back into some sort of order rather than dwelling on what might have been.

And so, a few hours later, all my plans mapped out and settled, I was hurrying across the car park behind the Fairview on my way to see Karen.

There was just enough light from the rear window of the main reception to guide me through the alley and at the far end, I reached for the door handle in the dark.

And gripped thin air.

The door was ajar.

Intense unease welled up inside me. Something was wrong.

I took a closer look.

The door had been forced. The strike plate was hanging loose on one screw and the wood where it had once been set in place was splintered and broken.

I steadied myself with one hand pressed against the cold damp wall while the hammering in my chest subsided. Karen was alone. Or at least, she should have been. And whoever had done this sure as hell wasn't paying a courtesy call.

I checked around me, peering into the darkness, senses ready to catch the smallest movement or the slightest sound. All was quiet. Gripping the edge of the door to stop it from swinging, I opened it slowly, careful not to let it creak, and stepped into the dimly lit hall. A thin strip of light leaked out from under the door to Karen's private quarters. The passage to the left was barely illuminated by the night-light from the main reception area beyond.

I pressed an ear to the inner door. The only sound was that of my heart thudding against my rib cage.

With one fist clenched, I rubbed the sweating palm of my other hand on my jeans, grasped the door handle, squeezed it gently, and pushed open the door, muscles taut, ready for whatever I might find on the other side.

Again, nothing. No sign of Karen or anyone else in the sitting room. The gas fire hissed. Its feeble light cast an eerie glow across the hearth, pushing back the darkness. An open book lay on the small occasional table near an armchair.

Still holding onto the door handle, I relaxed slightly.

Somewhere in the distance, a car backfired.

My muscles convulsed, a reflex action, and I jerked the door toward me, banging my head on the wooden frame. Breaking through that grim silence, the sound was like a thunderclap echoing through the rooms.

That was so fucking dumb.

I forced my muscles to relax and steadied myself against the door. I had to stay calm, not let my nerves get the better of me.

I waited, listening intently for any possible reaction to the sound.

Nothing. The darkness pressed in around me, brooding and silent.

I let go of the door, crept across the sitting room, and checked out the other rooms through the open doorways, the kitchen to the left and the ensuite bedroom to the right.

In the kitchen, the fluorescent glow of a street lamp, filtered by the semi-opaque blinds lent a dull jaundiced sheen to the metal pans dangling from a hanging rack by the window. Over in the far corner, the refrigerator purred. All else was silent.

The soft tread of my shoes on the parquet floor was the only other sound as I crept over to the bedroom doorway and checked the room for signs of movement. A double bed stood against the far wall flanked on both sides by matching bedside cabinets. A bank of wardrobes ran along the length of the room on the wall opposite the window and, at the other end of them, the open door to the bathroom. In the half-light, the large pieces of furniture appeared like dark slumbering beasts crouching in the shadows, silent and still.

But where was Karen? At this time of evening, she should be here, in her quarters.

I made my way back to the outer passage and followed it into the central reception area. The night-light cast a dim amber glow around the room, giving it a strange sombre look.

I was halfway across the room, heading towards the bar.

A scream rang out.

Behind me.

A long high wailing sound cut through the dead dense silence, reverberating around the building, and echoing back from the nearby walls.

I spun around towards it.

Towards the stairs.

And watched in horror as Karen, appearing from the darkness like a wraith, her mouth open and screaming, fell towards me, tumbling down the stairs in a broken heap and landing with a dull thud and the pistol crack of snapping bone onto the wooden floor below.

"Karen!" I cried out and ran towards her.

She tried to raise herself, pushing herself from the floor with one hand, her face a mask of pain. She shrieked again, a piercing sound that ripped through the room.

I dropped to my knees and reached out to her.

"Look out!"

The warning came too late. A dim shape emerged from the darkness and a boot struck me in the stomach, sending me sprawling across the floor. Searing pain shot through my body and I lay winded as a dark figure brushed past me and headed for the back door, disappearing from sight.

Fighting back the pain and with one hand clutching my bruised stomach muscles, I pulled myself across the floor towards Karen.

I reached her and she tried to push herself up on one elbow but cried out again and fell back to the floor. "Oh, God. I think my leg's broken."

"Don't try to move." I dug into my jeans pocket for my mobile and dialled the emergency services.

CHAPTER FORTY-THREE

Lowe said, "Don't try to move."

I pushed myself to my feet and stepped back as he dropped to his knees at Karen's side. His face was ashen.

"Are you okay?" he asked.

He had been the first to arrive, quickly followed by Nathan and two constables.

Karen's face twisted in pain. "It's my leg." She lay with her head on my folded up coat, her leg bent beneath her at an odd angle.

Lowe ran a practised eye over her prone form and winced when he saw the position of the limb.

"The ambulance is on its way," I offered.

Behind me, Nathan gave out directions to his men, sending them to check out the building for signs of disturbance. He joined us as Karen was relating what had happened and nodded a greeting. I ignored it and turned away. I wasn't feeling well disposed towards him.

"I heard a noise," Karen said. "All the guests were away. I went to check and found the back door open."

"It had been forced," I interjected.

Lowe acknowledged my input.

In between sobs of pain, Karen managed to recount how she had heard a sound from the reception and gone to take a look around. Finding nothing untoward and about to return to her room, she had spotted the guest register on the reception desk. "I never leave it there," she said. "I always keep it under the counter."

Nathan went to the desk and examined the register as Karen continued.

She explained how, hearing a noise from upstairs where the guest rooms are, she had gone to investigate.

"I took a look around the upper floor. Everything seemed okay, so I made my way back. He must have heard me and been waiting in the recess at the top of the stairs." She tried to move her leg and cried out in pain.

Lowe winced again and said, "It's best to stay still till the medics have checked you out." He took a handkerchief from his pocket and wiped her brow.

Karen went on. "I was pushed from behind. And the next thing I knew, I was at the bottom of the stairs. That's when I saw Mikey. I tried to warn him."

At that moment, we were interrupted by the sound of a siren and, minutes later, a couple of paramedics were kneeling over Karen, shooing us away.

I stood to one side, helpless, looking on as they checked her respiration and pulse, prompting her for details of injuries.

Officers and medics carried on with their duties around me and in the midst of all that activity, I stood transfixed, unable to tear my gaze from the prostate figure at my feet. The initial shock of the attack was wearing off and, as the implications and consequences of what had happened filtered through to my conscious mind, something else stirred and grew in me; a cold hard anger. It took hold of me and increased by degrees until I was gripped by a rage that set my whole body trembling.

How dare some anonymous piece of trash hurt a person I loved with such casual indifference. I wanted to lash out, hurt whoever had done this, smash everything within reach.

"Mikey?" Nathan took hold of my arm. "Let's go talk in the office."

The muscles in my arm went rigid at his touch and I recoiled, pulling away from him. I shook my head, unable to speak, still staring down at Karen.

"She'll be okay," Nathan said. He took my arm again. "Come on. Let them do their job."

I stiffened again but this time I let him lead me away. He guided me by the arm into the office behind the reception. My mind was whirring, full of strong conflicting emotions; rage, frustration, helplessness, fear. But mostly rage.

"Here, Mikey. Sit here."

I lowered myself in an armchair, my stomach muscles still

bruised and sore, and gripped the arms of the chair, digging my fingers into the fabric, staring straight ahead without seeing anything. There was just that white hot rage.

"Did you touch anything?"

Did I touch anything? What sort of inane question was that? My closest friend had been attacked and badly hurt. Could have been killed. And I was being asked if I'd touched anything.

I stared into the familiar face of the man I thought I had known, the man who had finally deceived me, and all that anger exploded out of me. "What sort of fucking stupid question is that?"

I knew how dumb this was, how inappropriate it was in the circumstances, but I couldn't stop myself. I was way beyond anger now.

"My best friend is lying broken on the floor and you want to know if I touched anything? She could have been killed and you want to know if I touched anything? Of course I fucking did. Would you like a list?"

"Calm down, Mikey. She's going to be all right. She has a broken leg and some cuts and bruises. But she's going to be okay."

"Oh, really? She's going to be okay is she?" I was shouting now. "She's going to get over being assaulted in her own home is she? She's going to get over nearly being killed by some maniac is she?"

He leaned toward me, a hand outstretched as though to touch me, but changed his mind and dropped the hand into his lap.

He said, "I understand how upsetting this is. Karen is my friend too. But right now I need you to tell me what happened. The sooner we get the facts, the sooner we can get moving on this."

"What the hell am I supposed to tell you that Karen hasn't already?

"A description would help."

"What? You think I had time to look him over while he was kicking the crap out of me? Really? You think maybe I had time to make a few notes while Karen lay there helpless and in pain?"

"Listen to me, Mikey. Whoever did this went through the hotel register. The only conclusion I can draw from that is that he was looking for a specific room. And the register is open at the page displaying your details."

"You're still saying this had something to do with me?"

"You have to be connected somehow. To all these recent events. You need to have a good hard think about this. I need something to go on."

He was looking to me for answers? My lip curled. "What the fuck is this? You're laying this on me? I'm the excuse for your incompetence am I?"

"Calm down, Mikey." The strain showed in his voice. He was struggling to keep an even tone but I didn't give a damn. I wasn't going to be used as a convenient scapegoat.

"No I won't fucking calm down. He could have killed her. You're the one who's supposed to protect us. So what are you doing about it? How many more people have to die before you get your act together?"

"This isn't helping. Come on, Mikey. Take a few deep breaths and calm yourself. Think about what happened and tell me as much as you can."

"I don't know what happened. How many times do I have to tell you?"

"Look, Mikey, you're upset. You're not thinking clearly. Maybe we can go through this again later. See if anything comes to mind."

"Of course I'm fucking upset. Some of us still have feelings."

"Okay, that's enough." He rose to his feet. "I'm going to drive you home. We can go through all this later when you've had a chance to think about it rationally."

"Rationally? So now I'm being irrational? I've just witnessed my friend nearly being killed, and you're accusing me of being irrational?" I didn't wait for a response. Dismissing him with a wave of the hand, I followed his example and stood up. "You needn't bother giving me a lift thanks. I can find my own way home."

"I'm trying to help you here, Mikey."

"Why would you?"

"Because we're friends and I'm concerned about you."

That was the last straw. I'd had enough of his bullshit. And that was the one word he should not have used right then.

"Friends?" I laughed, a low chuckle at first but slowly building until I was laughing out loud. "Friends?" I was mocking him now. "We're not friends, Nathan. We're ex-lovers. Not the same thing at all. You're just someone I once knew a long time ago. And now I'm not sure I know you any more."

"Mikey?"

He looked hurt but I didn't care. My anger was at an all-time high and I was on a roll.

"Leave me be," I said, "and go home to your boyfriend. I'm sure he must be eagerly anticipating your return. I'm just sorry I ever got involved with you again."

I didn't give him a chance to respond. It's not like there was much he could say anyway. No excuses.

I turned on my heels and headed to the main door.

Outside, I stopped at the top of the steps leading down from the terrace and stared out into the darkness, into the vast unknown. Only the cold unblinking stars stared back.

The freezing night air bit through my sweater and sank into my flesh, chilling me to the bone and reminding me that my overcoat was lying on the reception floor.

I wrapped my arms around my chest and tried to rub some warmth into my body while I pondered on all that had just happened. Much as I hated to admit it, Nathan was right, of course. Somehow I was involved in all this. I just wished I knew how.

But nothing came to mind. Whoever was behind these murders was looking for something. And whoever it was thought I had it. And was desperate enough to kill and put lives at risk to get it.

I cast my mind back over the past few days, thinking through everything I had seen and done, trying to bring to mind anything that might point to the identity of the murderer. But I drew a blank. Most of my time had been spent going through my father's papers and there was nothing there out of the ordinary.

Behind me, the door creaked opened, bringing me back to the present.

"You're going to need this." It was Nathan. He was holding my coat.

I took it from him without speaking and put it on.

He said, "I want to explain. About Brandon."

I shook my head. "I don't want to know. It's your business. Your private affairs have nothing to do with me."

"Mikey?"

"I'm really not in the mood. I don't have time for this."

I left him standing on the veranda and walked into the night.

CHAPTER FORTY-FOUR

It was a grey start to the day with rain clouds already scuttling in from the north, dampening my mood as well as the air.

That morning, once I'd finished packing in readiness for the journey home, my priority had been to phone the hospital to check on Karen's condition. I used my official position to blag information from the ward sister, a cheery soul, who reassured me that Karen was comfortable, had slept well, and, apart from the broken leg and some bruising, had no other injuries and would be discharged later that day. I also learned that Lowe had spent the night at her bedside. Ever the knight in shining armour.

Next, and with some apprehension, I called Nathan. After the verbal battering I'd given him the night before, I wasn't expecting a warm greeting. And I was right. He was cordial enough, despite the steely edge to his voice, but he wasn't in a conversational mood and kept me on the phone barely long enough to make an appointment.

He was working at the Charwell station that day, not far from the hospital, so I would visit Karen first, rather than wait until she was back home, and then go on to see Nathan immediately afterwards.

Taking my leave of Karen would be the easier of my two farewells. Saying goodbye to Nathan, later, would be harder and I wanted to get it over as soon as possible.

Ostensibly, it was to be an official interview to go over the events of the previous night and make a formal statement. But I had some apologising to do too.

Despite Nathan's final rejection, despite his less than candid disclosure about his relationship with Brandon Barwell, despite everything, I didn't want to leave on bad terms.

Finding out about Barwell had angered me. And after last night, after all that had happened, I had lost it and exploded with anger. Not one of my better moments. Being angry about all that had happened between us on a personal level, maybe that could be justified. But questioning his abilities on a professional level, that was a whole different matter. As a professional myself, I should have known better. That had been wrong. And I needed to make amends.

My only other task before leaving for London would be to return Jonas Wainwright's toolbox. I still had it in the boot of the Elan - something that had slipped my mind during the dramatic events of the past couple of days.

I meant to return here briefly before setting off for London and as the drive back from Charwell would take me past his house at The Heights, I could drop it off on my way to town. It would be one less task to worry about before heading home.

With nothing left to delay me, I heaved the two suitcases off the kitchen table and carried them out to the front of the house where the Elan was parked.

Before locking the door behind me, and with some regret, I looked around the room that had been home for the past few days. Now, it was devoid of any signs of habitation. An empty sterile space. But, no doubt, it would soon be home to Nathan and Brandon and would have that lived-in look again, the cosy domestic centre of their shared lives together.

I didn't want to think about it.

Once I'd secured the door, I carried the cases to the Elan and packed them into the boot, pushing Jonas's toolbox to one side to make room.

That's when I noticed the plastic carrier bag tucked into one corner.

At first, I couldn't recall how it had got there and what it contained. It was a moment or so before I remembered. I'd filled two bags with old papers and odds and ends of stationery I'd found in my father's desk during my first visit to the vicarage. This one must have slipped down behind the spare wheel and I'd overlooked it.

I yanked it out from its hiding place and rummaged around inside it. The papers appeared to be mostly old receipts and correspondence but among them were documents that warranted more scrutiny; they may well be of importance to my father's executors.

Along with the papers, there were several other items of stationery; a stapler and two boxes of staples, a packet of rubber band plus a few loose ones, and several miscellaneous coins.

And a computer memory stick.

Puzzled, I took it out of the bag and stared at it, turning it over and over in my fingers. Why was a computer memory stick among my father's possessions? He didn't even have a computer. And what was it Giles Trivett had said? Something about hating all forms of modern technology. We had laughed about it. So what was this doing among his belongings? And what did it contain?

I slipped it into my pocket. The answers would have to wait. I'd check it out later along with the papers. Right now, I needed to be on my way.

On the drive to the hospital, I went over in my mind what I wanted to say to Nathan. I was still trying to figure it out at the end of my journey as I searched for a space in the hospital car park, and was no nearer to a solution by the time I reached the ward.

It was lunchtime and the combined aromas of plated food from the half-dozen or so beds wafted around the large open room vying for olfactory attention with the pungent pervasive odour of disinfectant. How I loved hospitals.

Karen was propped up in a chair by the side of her bed over by the window on the far of the ward, eating what looked like a very unappetising casserole, her plaster-encased leg raised on a footstool. She was in animated conversation with Lowe who sat on the edge of the bed. They were laughing, too engrossed in each other to see my approach. I sidestepped an elderly woman in a dressing-gown shuffling towards me with a mobile IV drip-stand in tow, negotiated my way around the lunch trolley and crossed towards them between the two rows of beds. A large bunch of red roses, still in their cellophane wrapping stood in a glass jug on Karen's bedside table. No need to guess who they were from.

As I reached the two of them, I said to Karen, "You seem remarkably cheerful for someone who just took the quick way down a flight of stairs."

They were both grinning like a pair of idiots and Karen said, "That was yesterday. Today is decidedly better." She discarded her half-empty plate, placing it on the locker by the bed, and ran a hand across her forehead, brushing her hair to one side.

"Must be something good to make up for yesterday. Have you won the lottery?"

"Much better than that," she said, pressing a hand to her throat.

"I'm intrigued," I said. "So what is this momentous event?"

"Oh, for God's sake, Mikey. Are you blind?" She raised her hand and waved it in front of my face.

That's when I spotted the ring. A solitaire diamond on her left hand. "You're engaged?"

I reached over to where some metal-frame chairs stood at the side of the bedside locker, dragged one of them over to the bed, sank into it and sat and stared at her, lost for words.

Lowe leaned over and clasped a hand on my shoulder, still grinning inanely and Karen said, "Well don't just sit there. Say something."

"I'm in shock," I said. "This is so unexpected. And to think, a few days ago you didn't even have a boyfriend."

"Oh shut up," she said, still smiling.

Lowe raised his eyebrows. "What?" He sounded puzzled.

"Private joke," I said.

Karen shot Lowe a sideways glance. "I would have preferred a more romantic setting for a proposal. Under a Parisian moon or watching a sunset over the Mediterranean Sea." She pulled a face. "What will everyone think when I tell them you proposed to me in a hospital?"

I said, "Tell them you were in bed at the time and let them draw their own conclusions."

They both laughed and Karen said, "Any more suggestions like that and you're off my party list."

But of course I wasn't going to be a part of their celebrations. After today, I wouldn't be a part of their lives anymore. Losing Nathan had other consequences. Dreams of a new beginning, starting again with the man I had once shared my life with would have meant coming home, reintegrating into the local community, renewing relationships with old friends. And now none of that was going to happen. The dream was over.

Karen must have read my expression. Some of the sparkle left her eyes and she said, "But you won't be there anyway, will you?"

I grimaced. "I'm going to have a lot of catching up to do when I get back home."

"Yes, of course," she said.

We both knew it was a lie. And we both knew why I couldn't stay. If I was going to get my life back on track, I had to make a clean break from my past. Maybe one day, when I'd had time to come to terms with losing Nathan, I would come back.

Lowe, of course, wasn't clued in to what was happening. He said, "London isn't that far. And I'm sure Karen can always find you a bed for the night if you need to stay over."

Karen put a hand on his arm and squeezed it. "Mikey's going to be snowed under when he gets back. I'm sure he can come visit once he's settled back into his routine at home."

"You can invite me down for the wedding," I said. "Just don't make it too soon."

Karen snorted. "Please. One thing at a time."

Smiling, I rose to my feet, ready to take my leave.

Karen's expression became serious again. "Look after yourself, Mikey."

We locked eyes for a moment, no words passing between us. But the silence said so much more.

"I'm going to be okay," I said, answering the unspoken question.

I left them sitting side by side, Karen, my oldest dearest friend, leaning against the bed, and her new fiance, still grinning, with Karen's arm across his thigh.

At the exit, I waved goodbye.

There are two kinds of goodbyes. Saying goodbye to Karen had been of the first kind, the more usual and sometimes casual leave-taking of those you'll see again and, difficult though such goodbyes can sometimes be, they did not compare with the second kind for the heartache and pain they can cause. Saying goodbye to Nathan was of the second kind, the final farewell, and my heart was already sinking as I headed towards it.

CHAPTER FORTY-FIVE

Nathan greeted me with a brisk nod and said, "Take a seat, Mikey."

Clearly ill at ease, he'd adopted that cold formal tone he always did when he was being less than friendly. Stern faced, he stood behind the black leather swivel chair on the other side of his desk, gripping the backrest with both hands like a shield, as if defending himself. Perhaps he expected another outburst.

My cheeks burned with embarrassment at having put him in this position and I had to force myself to meet his gaze. He deserved better than my unwarranted and totally disproportionate criticism of the way he had handled this investigation. I needed to put it right.

As I took the offered seat, I cleared my throat and said, "Before we start, I owe you an apology. I had no right to say the things I did last night. I'm truly sorry. It was unforgivable."

Nathan visibly loosened up. The clenched jaw relaxed and he released his grip on the back of the chair.

"No need." He drew back the chair and sank into it. "It was understandable. You were upset." In the circumstances, his response was generous.

"That's no excuse. I should never have questioned your competence. You're doing all you can. I know that and I should have tried to be more helpful."

His handling of the investigation hadn't been my only criticism, of course. There was still the thorny issue of his failure to tell me about Brandon Barwell. But right now didn't seem the right time to raise the matter. Best to leave personal issues to one side.

There was a pile of manila files on the desk in front of him. He pushed it to one side and leaned forward, hands clasped. "You were distressed. And maybe I shouldn't have pushed you the way I did." He added, "I know it was a terrible thing to have happened but Karen is going to be all right. She's tough, always has been."

I acknowledged what he said and voiced my agreement. And

now, of course, Karen had more pleasant things to occupy her thoughts. He wouldn't have heard the good news yet but I'd let the happy couple have the pleasure of telling him. I wasn't in the mood for sharing good news about someone else's relationship; it made my own situation seem even more pathetic by comparison.

Nathan said, "Now you've had time to think about it, perhaps we can go over it again." His tone was more relaxed. Still formal - he was ever the professional when working - but his voice no longer had that brusque edge to it.

I sank back into my chair, relieved and more at ease. "I don't know what else I can tell you. It happened so quickly. There wasn't time to take it in." I cast my mind back and tried to conjure up an image of Karen's attacker. "I didn't get a good look at the guy. And I was crouched down at the time. But I'd say he was about my height. About six feet."

Nathan prompted some more. "This all helps. And I know you couldn't see his face. But what about his build? Anything you can tell me about his general appearance?"

I thought this over and said, "Nothing out of the ordinary. Well built I think." I tried to get a clearer picture of what happened in my mind." There is one thing," I added. "He was fit. The way he moved. He was agile."

"So that could give us an indication of his age?"

I affirmed. "Yes, I suppose so. If I had to make a guess, based on his build and the way he moved, I'd place him somewhere between late twenties to mid forties. And someone used to physical activity."

"Anything else? Did he speak?"

"Never said a word. Sorry, I can't tell you any more."

"You've already told me a lot. And it all helps. I'll have one of my officers go through the details with you and take down a formal statement. If you think of anything else though, do let me know."

"Sure, I will."

"There is something else, Mikey." There was another change in his tone. Hesitant. Uncertain. "I understand you're moving back to London."

"I presume Brandon told you?"

"He tells me he visited you."

"He's a nice guy. I enjoyed meeting him." Total lie of course but there was no point saying otherwise. The least I could do was accept defeat with good grace.

"I meant to tell you he was staying over. I wanted to find the right time."

The right time? Yeah, sure. Like there was a right time to tell your erstwhile lover he was being passed over for someone else.

I forced a smile and said, "There really is no need. It's none of my business. And I'll be leaving later today anyway."

His face creased into a look of concern and I almost believed he was disappointed as if he was sorry to see me go.

"It would help if you could stay around a while longer," he said. "I'm sure you'll appreciate that this investigation is far from over and we may need to interview you again."

So that was it. My leaving might impede his investigation. Nothing personal. He wasn't going to miss me at all.

I said, "I realise that so I'll leave my contact details at the desk. But I really do have to get back. Lots to do. And it's not as if I'm so far away I can't get back at short notice."

He made a half-hearted protest but I made it clear I wasn't going to change my mind.

"And besides," I said, "I need ..." I searched for the right words. "The past few days have been difficult. I need to get away." I added, "From Elders Edge."

Of course he knew what I really meant. I needed to get away from him. And so in the end, he acquiesced; there wasn't much else he could do.

He rose to his feet, interview over, and said, "I'll walk you over to the desk and find someone to take your formal statement. But before I do, I wanted to wish you well for the future. Lowe is going to take over the day-to-day running of the investigation so he'll be the one getting in touch if we need to see you again."

He held out a hand.

So that was it. Just a handshake. A formal goodbye. I wanted more than that. I wanted to reach out and hug him, hold him close and tell him how sorry I was for all the hurt I'd caused him and how much I regretted losing him. But I knew that if I did, I'd get emotional and make a fool of myself. This way was best.

I took his hand and shook it.

"And we can still be friends," he said.

I gave his hand an extra squeeze. "Of course we can."

But of course we couldn't. I took a good long look at him, knowing I was seeing him for the last time.

This was the image of him I would take with me. A tall confident man dressed in regulation grey flannel suit and white shirt which did little to hide that proud erect body, a lopsided smile creasing his face.

How I would miss him. I hoped that he was happy at last, that he had found what he was looking for. And I wished him well. But we couldn't be friends. I'd already lost the best part of him and I couldn't settle for less. I was saying goodbye for the last time.

CHAPTER FORTY-SIX

Even Axwell and Ingrosso's upbeat rendition of "Sun is Shining" failed to raise my spirits. I switched off the car radio and drove the rest of the way to Wainwright's house in silence. Saying goodbye to Nathan had put me out of sorts and the last thing I needed was an endless stream of bright cheery music to depress me even more.

Wainwright wasn't in a particularly upbeat mood either. He was surprised to see me until he saw I was carrying his toolbox.

"I'd almost given up on getting that back," he said."

I ignored the implied criticism. "Well you have it now."

He held up a pair of grease-stained hands. "I was just tinkering with the car. Could you bring it through to the kitchen?"

He wasn't very welcoming but I followed him into the house anyway. He led me through the living room towards the back of the house. The air was musty and the faint odoriferous smell of garbage drifted in from the kitchen. A stein of beer stood on a small coffee table by the fireplace, the table's dull surface scarred by coffee cup rings.

I didn't suppose domestic hygiene was one of Jonas's priorities right then and I guessed he'd let things slide without Erin to take care of the domestic chores. Not that I blamed him for that. He'd had enough to contend with.

The living room was dominated by a large old-fashioned fabric-covered three-piece suite with a faded floral design in muted shades of yellow. Laura Wainwright sat with her back to me in one of the overstuffed chairs watching a large black-framed flat-screen TV over a faux-marble mantelpiece. It was an incongruous modern touch in this setting.

The TV was tuned to a recording of a reality TV talent show blaring out an off-key attempt at a Metallica song by a singularly unattractive band of goths who looked like they would be more at home in a funeral parlour. I gave it a zero.

Laura tore herself away from the screen long enough to see who was passing by. She flushed and quickly turned away when she realised who it was.

After the episode with the bracelet, I doubted I was one of her favourite people right then. Poor kid. After all she'd been through, not only losing her mother but also having to cope with Erin's tragic death, I had mixed feelings about having exposed her pilfering. I regretted adding to her considerable woes by being yet another source of distress.

Wainwright took me through to the kitchen and I carried the toolbox over to the table while he washed his hands at the sink.

He wasn't in a talkative mood and neither was I. So, after a few desultory exchanges, I made my excuses, pleading the need to set off for London as soon as possible, and made my way out.

He saw me to the door and I was about to take my leave when a battered old Renault Megane drew up to the gate, and out stepped Giles Trivett.

As he turned towards the house, our eyes met and he stopped in his tracks, hesitant, as if unsure to continue. I'd be one of the last people he'd want to see given the part I'd played in exposing his wife's infidelity. Meeting unexpectedly like this would have embarrassed him. He stared at me, dull-eyed, from behind his thick-lensed spectacles before dropping his gaze and making his way towards us along the garden path. He walked slowly as if weighed down by a heavy load, all his natural exuberance gone.

Irrational though it was, I experienced a pang of guilt. I felt partly responsible for his current circumstances. And, of course, news of Frances Trivett's affair and possible prosecution for wasting police time wouldn't enhance his reputation. It wasn't the sort of image befitting a clergyman. Learning of his wife's infidelity and duplicity would have been a bitter blow.

As he approached, he avoided any further eye contact with me. Someone else who'd crossed me off their favourite persons' list. Two in one day. It was enough to make a lesser man paranoid.

He addressed himself to Wainwright and said, "I need to speak with you about the outstanding repairs at the vicarage." Shooting me a sideways glance, he added, "but I can come back later if you're busy."

That was the only acknowledgement I got.

I butted in. "We're finished here so I'll leave you to it."

He answered with a brief nod.

"There is one thing before I go." I spoke to Trivett. "I found another batch of papers among my father's possessions. If any of them relate to his estate, I'll drop them off later."

"No need." He spoke sharply and looked decidedly aggrieved. Probably didn't want me bumping into Frances. "Leave them at reception and I'll pick them up from the Fairview later."

"I'm not at the Fairview. I have a holiday let over on Fleming Road. It's not far from the vicarage so it'll be no bother to drop them off."

I turned to go, cutting short his stammered objections, and then remembered the memory stick. "One other thing." I took the stick out of my pocket as I turned back to him and held it up. "This was among the papers. Not sure why my father would have it. It's not yours is it?"

He shook his head. "I've not seen it before."

"It was a long shot. I thought maybe it was church records of some kind."

His reply was curt. "No, sorry." He sounded like he didn't care one way or the other.

I shoved the stick back into my pocket. It would have to wait until later. Right then, I wanted to get away.

All three of them; Wainwright, Laura and Trivett, had good cause to be in low spirits. But as much as I sympathised with them, I was depressed enough about my own sorry situation without having to endure any more of their mournful company.

CHAPTER FORTY-SEVEN

Back at Barwell's place, I'd only just made it through the door when Jerry called. Something about a contract for a book deal he needed to discuss. It was a timely reminder I had a living to make and couldn't afford to let things slide. Besides which, throwing myself back into work would take my mind off my current troubles.

While we talked, I unpacked the laptop from my messenger bag and set it up on the kitchen table. I booted it up and, once I'd finished the call - promising Jerry I would be back in London later that day - I settled myself in front of it and inserted the memory stick.

I hadn't been totally convinced by Trivett's inability to recognise the memory stick. After all, his mind was on more pressing concerns right then. And if the stick contained official documents, as I suspected it might, I would need to make sure it was in Trivett's possession before I left Elders Edge.

A number of files flashed up on the screen, most of them identified by a number.

I opened the file marked "7".

It took me a moment to realise what I was looking at. And when I did, my stomach heaved and a sour taste filled my mouth. I stared in horror at the images that filled the screen and my throat tightened.

I'm not sure what I'd expected to find, maybe scanned copies of more household receipts and a mix of documents, but not this. I presumed that the figure '7' identifying the file referred to the ages of the young girls whose photos were contained in it. So many of them. A lot of them naked. And all posed in positions that, in an adult, might have been defined as provocative.

Some of them weren't alone. Some of them ... I closed down the file, unable to look at it any more.

I shut my eyes, and kept them shut, taking in some long deep breaths to slow my racing heart. My mouth dried, and the tightness in my throat turned to a burning sensation.

From somewhere in the distance came the faint hum of traffic and the occasional blast of a horn as the rest of Elders Edge went about their daily lives. Inside the room, the grim silence was broken by the slow sonorous ticking of the clock on the mantle.

I opened my eyes and took another look at the screen. One of the files was named with the initials "LW" rather than a number. I opened it with a trembling hand. It contained more images of a similar kind. But these were of just one girl. A thirteen year old. I knew that because I knew the girl. It was Laura Wainwright.

I cried out, an involuntary squawk, and slammed the laptop shut, pushed it away, and buried my face in my hands, trying to blank those images from my mind.

My stomach knotted, and I swallowed hard to stop the bile rising in my throat.

It was several minutes before I raised my head again.

There had to be some connection between what I'd found in those files and all that had happened over the past few days, and now that I'd overcome my initial shock, I thought back to those recent events and tried to place them together into some semblance of a pattern.

Was there a Paedophile ring in Elders Edge? Was there something that rotten at the very heart of this simple and seemingly benign community?

If so, how was it linked to the recent murders? Had it been uncovered and had someone killed to protect it from exposure? Was blackmail involved?

Or was it just one person? A not-so-respectable member of the local population? And what part did my father play in all this?

Dear God, please don't let it be him. Anything but that. Such a possibility didn't bear thinking about.

And Black? What was his role?

And what of Laura Wainwright? Had she been groomed, taken advantage of whilst still emotionally vulnerable after losing her mother? Was she still in the clutches of whoever had taken these photos? Is that why Erin Colby had died? Because she had found out?

So many unanswered questions. So many possibilities. One thing seemed certain, someone had been desperate enough to risk discovery to get their hands on this memory stick. If it had fallen into the hands of the police and the girls identified, it wouldn't have been long before the whole sordid secret was uncovered and the perpetrators, whoever they were, brought to justice with all that it implied. No wonder someone may well have murdered to get it back.

A cold tingle ran down my spine.

I pulled the memory stick from the laptop and stared at it as if it could give me some answers.

Behind me, a draught of cold air. And a floorboard creaked. A voice said, "I've been looking for that."

A shock of adrenaline surged through me and I whirled around, rising to my feet, muscles taut.

It was Wainwright. Standing by the open back door on the other side of the room. He must have followed me back here as soon as he'd got rid of Trivett.

I froze. "You have a gun?" A rather inane question in the circumstances. He quite clearly had a gun. It was pointing straight at me.

CHAPTER FORTY-EIGHT

Wainwright flipped the gun at me and pushed the door to behind him. "In my line of work, pest control can be a bit of a problem. All those sites to be cleared. Unfortunately, I've had to get rid of a few human pests recently."

"You?"

"Yes, me." Behind the beard, his face was hard set.

"I don't understand."

I did understand. Only too well. My life was at risk. And I needed to figure a way out of what was now a dangerous situation. I had to think fast.

"What's to understand?" He said. "Scum like Black deserve all they get."

"Black?"

I was still holding the memory stick. He pointed down at it with his gun. "Who do you think took those photos you have there?"

I slipped the stick into my pocket. "So you killed him?"

"Damn right I did. After what he did to Laura, I have no regrets about that."

From where I stood, there was just a chance I could move fast enough to disarm him. He'd kept some distance between us before announcing himself, but if I kept him talking while his gun was still lowered, maybe I could do it.

"How did you find out?" I shifted my weight forward onto one foot and wrapped a hand around the narrow top rail of the chair I'd just vacated.

He relaxed his stance, lowered the gun even more. "I followed her. I knew she was up to something. Sneaking off all the time."

His eyes were no longer focused, his mind elsewhere.

Now was my chance.

Tightening my grip on the chair, I wretched it from the floor and lunged forward.

It caught against the table.

I gasped and stumbled.

Jonas snapped to attention and jerked the gun up again. "Nice try," he snarled. "Now get back."

I regained my balance and hesitated. Perhaps I was close enough to risk it, go for him.

"Back." He barked the order at me and pointed the gun directly at my head.

My chance had gone. No point arguing. I stepped back. Now I needed to buy some time while I figured out my options. I had to keep him talking.

"No one could blame you for what you did," I said. If I could show him I was on his side, that I sympathised with him, maybe I could help to change his mood, put him in a more reasonable frame of mind and talk him out of doing anything reckless. "Any father would have done the same."

In response, he laughed, a harsh bitter sound. "Pity your father didn't share your opinion."

"My father? How did he get involved?"

"You can blame my daughter for that. She took it into her head to confess. She went to see him the following day and told him the whole thing."

She must have watched while Wainwright beat Black half to death in a mindless rage and then throttled the life out of him. Any wonder that she would turn to my father, the person who had given her comfort and support following her mother's death. Anyone would have been traumatised by such events, let alone a vulnerable child.

I said, "Is that how he got the photos?"

"Yes. Unfortunately for him. He called me. Told me I had to go to the police. Wouldn't take no for an answer." He shook his head. "He should have stayed out of it. But he always had to take the moral high road, didn't he? And everything was black and white. No shades of grey. Any decent person would have turned a blind eye."

Personally, I couldn't think of any decent person who would turn a blind eye to murder. But what would I know? Wainwright obviously moved in different circles. Probably best to let it pass.

"So he had to die too?"

I surreptitiously scanned the room while I kept him talking, looking for something to use as a weapon. Anything.

Over to my left, a small lamp stood on a side table by the main door. It was the only object in an otherwise spartan room that may have served as a weapon. I tried to judge the distance to the door. It was too far. I would never make it in time.

At my side, to the right, a floor-standing shelving unit stood against the wall but all it contained were an empty photo frame, some glass ornaments and a few paperback books, nothing of any use.

The only other objects that may have served were a set of cast iron saucepans hanging on a rack over the sink by the back door. But they were out of reach behind Wainwright.

He was still talking. "I agreed to go and see him so he could accompany me to the police station and give me some support. Of course, I never intended to let it get that far. He's already called Erin to put her off coming. Some excuse about having a cold. So we weren't likely to be disturbed. And he was frail. Disposing of him wasn't difficult. He didn't put up much of a struggle."

My blood ran cold. Wainwright had killed Black in a fit of rage. And though it had been a grisly act, it had at least been understandable. But this. This was beyond understanding. The way he described killing my father was so matter-of-fact. Almost casual. It was chilling.

And if he could kill with such indifference, it made my own current predicament even more dangerous than I had realised. But I had to keep him talking, try to give myself some time to figure a way out of this.

I dug the memory stick out of my pocket and held it up. "You went to a lot of trouble to get your hands on this. You could have just taken it from my father at the time."

"If I'd known about it, I would have. I'm not stupid. Laura didn't think to tell me about it till later." He curled his lip. "It caused me a lot of grief hunting that thing down."

"Well now it's all yours," I said and threw it to the floor at his feet.

I'd hoped he might stoop down to pick it up, giving me a chance to go for him. But no such luck. Clearly, he wasn't going to risk being caught off guard again. He didn't even glance down. Just kept the gun levelled at me.

I was running out of options.

But I had an idea.

There was a slim chance I would pull it off, but I needed to keep him occupied while I worked out my moves.

I said, "And the argument my father had with Black? What was that about?"

Wainwright snorted. "It never happened. When Trivett saw me coming out of the vicarage, I made the whole thing up. If I could get everyone to believe Black had disappeared after arguing with your father, suspicion would have fallen on him."

"Clever move. And I guess it was you who sent the text message to the surgery from his mobile?"

"Yes. And, it might have worked too if you hadn't found Black's body. Though it did have the added advantage of covering my tracks if anyone had spotted my van the previous day. I drove back to Black's with my tools later that day to dig his grave."

Some more of the pieces fell into place.

The vicarage porch would have obscured Giles Trivett's view of the door. So the day he spotted Wainwright stepping out of it, he couldn't have known that Wainwright had left the house itself and then passed off his visit as an unsuccessful attempt to rouse my father.

I shuddered. Wainwright must have killed my father minutes before and yet had still managed to appear calm and controlled enough to pass off his presence there as a casual visit.

"You had it all so well planned, didn't you?"

"And I have no intention of letting you or anyone else screw it up now. You really shouldn't have interfered."

It was time to act. Feigning a sudden loss of energy, I let my legs buckle under me before regaining my balance, pushing myself back to my feet, and leaning over against the shelving unit to my right.

"Stay where you are." Wainwright followed me with the gun.

"Please. I feel faint." I reached out and grabbed hold of one of the unit's uprights as if to steady myself. I tested its rigidity with my hand. It wobbled slightly.

"It will all be over soon," he said, raising the gun. "I didn't want to do this. But you have only yourself to blame." He took aim.

It was now or never. Using every ounce of strength I had, I pulled the rickety shelving around towards him and slammed my shoulder hard against it, sending it hurtling in his direction.

The flimsy shelving crashed to the floor in front of him, it contents flying in all directions.

Wainwright jumped back instinctively, narrowly avoiding the unit and ducking away from a glass ornament that smashed into the wall. He fell against the sink unit behind him, grunted, momentarily winded, and dropped the gun.

Now was my chance. Pushing back on one foot, I threw myself across the room. I landed, full length, on the wooden floor and reached for the gun.

A few inches too short. I stretched out, straining to reach the weapon, my hand clutching spasmodically at the air.

Not close enough.

The steel-capped toe of a boot struck my shoulder hard, knocking me, yelling, across the floor. My head slammed against the table by the main door.

Bursts of orange light filled with searing pain blinded me as I rolled over and pushed myself to my knees. I raised my head and, through the pounding pain, stared up into the barrel of Wainwright's gun inches from my face.

"That wasn't very bright," he said.

"You won't get away with this. Someone was sure to have seen you come here."

He shook his head. "Once I'd spotted your car outside, I

parked up around the corner and came through the woods at the back. No one saw me. I made sure of that."

He stood back, stretched out his arm, and took aim again.

"I didn't want to harm anyone," he said, "but I'm not going to let Black ruin my life. Why should I have to suffer for what he did?"

"You don't have to do this." I kept my voice calm and even. I had nothing left now but words and all I could do was try to persuade him not shoot me. "No one could blame you for what you did to Black. And everything that followed could be explained by your state of mind. I've been involved in enough court cases to know the score in situations like this. You were of unsound mind. It would be a viable defence."

Wainwright's shook his head and sneered. "Maybe I could get away with killing Black. But not your father. And certainly not Erin."

My breath caught in my throat. "You killed her too?"

"Once I'd figured Black would have copies of the photos on his laptop, I went back for it. She found it. Thought it was Laura's. She thought she'd be doing me a favour checking Laura's emails and files. Keeping tabs on her. Big mistake. She called me at work."

That must have been why she called me. For advice. When she couldn't get through to me, she must have called him instead. If I'd been able to take the call, she might still be alive.

"She broke away when I went for her," he said. "Panicked and made a run for it. Just my good luck she'd come over in her car. Made it so much easier."

There was no emotion in his voice as he spoke. It was as if he were relating some ordinary everyday event.

"There's still a chance of pleading a good case. You can still beat this."

Of course, I knew he couldn't. He'd gone too far down that slow easy road to hell, abandoning all sense of morality bit by bit along the way. And what had started as the frenzied but understandable murder of someone who had violated his daughter had ended as the callous calculated murder of innocent people. He must have known that too. There was no argument I could make to persuade him otherwise and, in that moment, I knew that my death was inevitable. There was nothing more to say.

It was strange how calm I felt, knowing my life was about to end.

So this was to be my final resting place. This cold hard floor. No doubt I would share Black's fate and be buried somewhere in the woods.

I stared up into the barrel of the gun and waited for the inevitable.

His finger pressed against the hammer.

"Don't be a fool, Wainwright."

A movement in the doorway.

It was Nathan.

He stepped into the room over the shattered remains of the shelving unit, his eyes fixed on Wainwright.

My first reaction was one of overwhelming relief. I'd never been so glad so see him. Till it occurred to me that his position here was no less perilous than mine. This could end badly for both of us.

Slowly, I pushed myself up from the floor. My head still throbbed. I rose to my feet.

Wainwright backed away into the corner of the room, putting some distance between both of us and himself, and pointed the gun first at me and then at Nathan. He waved it toward me. "Move over there. I want you standing together."

Nathan stood his ground. "I'm going nowhere. This is over, Wainwright."

"Not for me it's not. But it is for you. You're not going to take me. And what difference does one more body make now." He raised the gun and pointed it at Nathan.

Talking was over. Nathan was about to die. And I wasn't going to let that happen. This was the man I loved, the man whose life meant more to me than my own. Even if I'd been destined never to see him again, I would have been content to know that he was safe and living a full and happy life.

But not this. Not this.

And with one long anguished cry, I launched myself at Wainwright.

He whipped around to face me, his eyes wide with surprise. But it wasn't enough to slow him. The distance between us was too great.

He raised the gun and fired.

A blinding flash, and my world was filled with raw unbearable searing pain. I fell to the floor. The last thing I saw was Nathan struggling with Wainwright. And then darkness closed in and the world went away.

CHAPTER FORTY-NINE

"You fucking stupid bonehead. Were you out of your fucking mind?"

Never one to mince his words, Nathan was as forthright as ever. And he was blazing. But for once I couldn't respond; I was too shocked. He was a mess. The usually strong firm face was pale and drawn. And dark circles beneath red-rimmed eyes betrayed his lack of sleep. I bit my lip and shook my head.

He used my silence to kick off again.

"What the hell were you thinking of? Are you really that dumb?"

Maybe I should have let it pass but I wasn't in the mood for this. I was back in hospital. Never somewhere to bring out the best in me. Even the private room didn't help. I was already impatient and tetchy before he showed up and now he was aggravating my mood.

Pulling my robe around me, I rose from the bedside chair and stepped towards him. "Well strange as it may seem, I didn't want you getting killed."

"It's my job to take those sorts of risks, Mikey."

"That's okay then," I snapped. "When we finally bury you, I can always console myself with the thought that you were just doing your job."

He stepped towards me, clenching and unclenching his hands. "I could have handled it. Have you any idea how close you came to having your brains blown out? Always presuming you have any. Do you know how lucky you are?"

I didn't feel lucky. My head still throbbed from where Wainwright's bullet had grazed my skull, my hair had been shaved off, and the bandage around my head made me look like something out of 'The Mummy'.

I said, "He was about to put a bullet through you. What else was I supposed to do?"

Suddenly, it was all too much. Tired, exhausted, and drained of energy, I couldn't cope with this.

Through a blur of tears, I cried out, "Why are you treating me like this? What did I do that was so wrong?"

All those strange mixed-up emotions that had built up inside me over the past few days were becoming too much to contain. Like the pressure of water building up against the wall of a dam, I could no longer hold back the torrent that was about to be unleashed. The dam wall was crumbling. And as it fell away, a flood of pain and anguish poured out and I could no longer control it.

Crying openly, I sank onto the edge of the bed and shouted out, "I love you, you fucking idiot. And I didn't want to have to go to your funeral. Is that okay with you?"

He blanched. "Say that again."

"With the greatest of pleasure. You're a fucking idiot."

"The other bit."

I hadn't meant to blurt out my feelings like that. It was so pointless. Blinking back my tears, I said, "Why? You want me to make an even bigger fool of myself? Would that make you happy?"

"I just want you to talk to me." His voice was breaking up.

"That's rich coming from you." Choking back my sobs, I said, "When do you ever talk to me? I spent half my life trying to read your mind."

"You don't make it easy, Mikey. I don't know what you want."

Now the dam had burst, the raging waters were in full flow, unstoppable, spewing out a storm surge of all those pent up feelings I had repressed for far too long.

"I wanted you to forgive me." I spluttered out the words. "I wanted you to tell me everything was all right. Just like it used to be. I wanted you back, and I didn't know how."

"For God's sake, Mikey." He stepped over to the bed and sank down beside me.

Leaning towards me, he wrapped his arms around me and pulled me close, holding me tight against his chest. His hand cupped the back of my neck. "There are times I could cheerfully throttle you," he murmured.

My cheek was wet against his neck. "I didn't know what to do."

He pulled back and held me at arm's length. His expression had softened. "Here's an idea. Radical though it may seem, why don't we try talking to each other?"

"I wanted to. But then I found out about Brandon. And it was too late."

"Brandon's gone back to London. I won't be seeing him again." He reached up and ran a thumb under each of my eyes, wiping away the tears.

I said, "I don't understand."

He shook his head. "You know, Mikey, for someone in your line of work, you can be surprisingly dense at times." He slipped an arm around my waist. "Why do you think I'm so angry with you for nearly getting yourself killed? You think I would have found it any easier to deal with?"

I stared at him, uncomprehending, not sure what to say.

"I've had a lot to think about over these past few days. You coming back here. And then Brandon."

He paused for a moment as if gathering his thoughts and continued, "When he told me how he felt, what he wanted, I knew I had to let him go. Whatever vision of the future he imagined for us, it wasn't one I shared. We talked it over. And in the end, we both decided it would be for the best if we went our separate ways."

"He seemed so certain."

"I never made him any promises and I guess we had different needs. But it did make me think long and hard about what I did want."

"And what was that?"

He leaned away from me and stared directly at me, searching my face as if looking for something. "God knows you've not made it easy for me, Mikey. And there are times you've driven me to distraction. But there's never been anyone else. And when I thought I'd lost you ..." He closed his eyes and screwed them tight shut. "You have no idea what that was like."

I stared into his face, pained by the anguish I saw there. How had I got it so wrong? I was confused. "These last few days, you've been so distant. I thought you were pushing me away."

He turned away. "That night we spent together. I thought ... I hoped ..." He turned back to face me, his expression tense. "I tried to get you to open up. Tell me what you wanted."

He rose from the bed, crossed to the window, his back to me. "I didn't have an easy time of it letting you go. And when you came back, all those old feelings got stirred up again."

A pause.

The clashing sound of a trolley bed rattling across the courtyard drifted up from below, blending with the distant hum of traffic.

I waited in silence until he was ready to speak again. He slipped his hands into his pocket, the muscles in his broad shoulders rippling under the dark grey shirt.

Turning away from the window he said, "I couldn't go through all that again, Mikey. If you weren't serious ..." He broke off. "I couldn't go through it again."

I rose and crossed toward him. "I'm so sorry. I caused us both so much pain." I raised a hand and stroked his face. "So many wasted years." The tears welled up again.

He pressed his hand against mine and then took it in both his own and squeezed it. "What's past is past."

"And now?"

"I don't know about you but I don't want to go on living a life full of regrets. And if there is a chance for us, I'd like to take it."

"I ran away once before. It was the most stupid thing I ever did. I'm not running away again."

"Then it starts here. We start being honest with each. We talk through our problems. We find a way to make it work. Okay?"

"Okay," I said.

A moment later, I was back in his arms.

CHAPTER FIFTY

Lowe slid the statement across the desk. "Just needs signing, Mr MacGregor, and we're all done."

We were in his office. Again. It was becoming a habit.

I read through the document. "So where do we go from here?"

"He'll be charged with attempted murder."

I added my signature to the bottom of the statement and pushed it back to him. "On top of all the other charges, you have to wonder if it's worth the bother. Did he make a full confession?"

Lowe signed as witness and said, "In the case of Black, I'm not sure 'confession' is the right word. That would imply an expression of remorse. I think 'boast' would be a better word."

During that final showdown at Brandon's place, Wainwright had been no match for Nathan. Overpowered and restrained, he had been taken into custody, and once the full extent of his crimes had been exposed, he'd been left with no option but to come clean, pleading mitigating circumstances in the hope of moderating his punishment. But even then, he'd had no regrets about killing Black.

Lowe filled me in on the details. During his confession, he'd related how he had followed Laura to Black's house through the woods and when she had failed to come out, he'd peered through the window. Enraged at seeing her violated, he had forced his way in, beaten Black almost senseless and then strangled him in a final fit of fury.

And then the chilling details of Laura's abuse had been revealed. How Black had befriended and groomed her during her visits with Erin. How he had taunted her with the memory stick when she tried to break away from him, blaming her for leading him on and threatening to use the photos to expose her, convincing her that she was the one who would suffer the consequences. How she had stolen the memory stick from his desk drawer on that last day, hoping that by destroying it, she could get away from him. And how she had later passed it on to my father.

Ironically, Wainwright had found a far more effective means to end Black's abuse of his daughter. But, unfortunately, the consequences of his actions had also been far more extreme. The added psychological damage to his daughter being one of them. It had not occurred to him that far from protecting his daughter, he had damaged her fragile psyche even more, added to the psychological harm many times over.

"What about Laura," I asked. "How is she coping?"

Lowe's face fell. "Taking the girl's statement was no joyride. Social services were on hand to help her through it. But even so, I don't know how she'll get over it. There are always losers."

He sounded so dejected, I was almost sorry I'd asked. "Hey, come on. You have better things to occupy your mind right now."

He brightened up at that.

"And while we're on the subject, given that you've just got engaged to my closest friend, do you think we could drop the Mr-bloody-MacGregor thing? It's Mikey. Okay, Richard?"

He grinned. "Sounds good to me."

And then he became serious again. "And how about you and the Chief?"

"What?" That came out of nowhere.

"Karen told me you used to be - you know - more than just friends."

I was stuck for words. What was I supposed to say to that?

He said, "It's cool. I don't have a problem with it."

"Okay."

"The boss is a very private person. Not one for talking about his private life. But I used to see him around with that guy, Brandon. He never tried to hide anything."

I tried to keep the regret from my voice when I answered. "He always was a better man than me."

CHAPTER FIFTY-ONE

I checked both sides of my head in the mirror. My new razor cut hairstyle didn't look so bad.

"Does this suit me?" I said.

From behind me, Nathan said. "It's an improvement on your recent headgear. You looked like something out of ..."

I cut him short. "Thanks, but I don't need to know that."

It was the afternoon of Karen and Lowe's engagement party and Nathan had dropped by to pick me up on the way.

I'd brought up the subject of his staying over again. But he was still being cautious, wanting to take things a step at a time. Not that I minded so much. At least now we were both on the same wavelength. And the future was looking more positive.

The local Estate Agent had sent someone round that morning to erect a 'For Sale' sign at the front of the house. Brandon, it seemed, had cut his losses and chosen to move on. My bags were packed and in the boot of the car, ready for my drive back to London straight after the party.

Nathan was helping himself to a pre-party can of beer from the fridge, a luxury he allowed himself on one of his rare days off duty.

He said, "Was your agent okay with you staying on a while longer?"

I was still checking out my reflection. Perhaps this new hairstyle was a bit too severe.

"I told him I was being detained by the police."

In the mirror, I saw Nathan roll his eyes.

"Well, it's true," I said. "You did detain me."

He grunted. His usual way of showing disapproval.

"It's okay, I said. "He's cool. He knew I'd need a few days to recover. And I told him about the party. I'll have to drive back straight after though. I've a lot of catching up to do."

Nathan dropped onto the couch, opened the can and took several long swigs. I sat down beside him.

"I never got a chance to ask," I said. "What made you come

over that day? How did you know I was in trouble?"

"I didn't."

I must have looked confused. He said, "I wanted to talk to you about us. I didn't want to let you go without trying to put things right."

"So you had no idea what was happening?"

"None." He took another swig of beer. "When I reached the house, I could hear you talking with someone. I was just about to leave again."

"What changed your mind?"

"It was only then I realised you were in trouble." He drained the can and crushed it in his fist.

"How?"

He rose, crossed over to the waste-bin by the sink, and dropped the can in it. "Two reasons. First, I heard a crash. The shelving unit. So I knew something must be wrong. I couldn't see what was happening - the blinds were drawn - so I went round to the back and found the door ajar."

He glanced at his watch. "Are you ready? We should get moving."

"Sure," I said and grabbed my jacket from the back of the nearby armchair. "And the second reason?" I stood and put on the jacket.

"Well, that was the clincher," he said, heading for the door. "You interfered in the investigation all the way through. And as we both know, Mikey, whenever you choose to interfere in something that doesn't concern you, it usually leads to trouble."

I stopped short on my way to the door. "That's not what happened." I was indignant.

"Right. So being threatened at gunpoint by a homicidal maniac isn't trouble then?" He ushered me out of the door and closed it behind him.

I locked the door and handed him the keys. "Well, yes," I conceded. "In that particular circumstance."

He pocketed the keys and said, "Point made."

"It had nothing to do with ..." I stopped myself short and gave up the argument. I was wasting my breath. He'd always had a remarkable talent for finding ways to blame me for my own misfortunes. And for once, I had every reason to be grateful for his misguided presumption. I might not have been here to argue the point otherwise.

We drove to the Fairview in separate cars. Nathan was staying over that night and driving back home in the morning. And I was heading off to London later that day.

We met up again in the car-park behind the Fairview.

I crossed over to his Astra as he locked up and said, "What will happen to Laura?" She's been on my mind."

"That's up to social services. She has some other family. Grandparents. So I suppose they'll be involved."

"That girl. What she must have been through."

"So much for a father who wanted to protect his child. He ended up destroying everything she had."

"I hope it works out for her."

On that sombre note, we made our way to the party.

Karen was brimming over with curiosity about my decision to stay on for her celebration. I knew she would be.

"You came together?" she said, greeting us at the door. Ever hopeful.

"We met in the car park," said Nathan.

The disappointment on her face was obvious.

I leaned over and kissed her cheek. "Might have something to tell you later, " I whispered. "But this is your day, so it can wait."

Before she had a chance to object or press me for an explanation, I left her in the company of Nathan and went to find Lowe to congratulate him again.

It was a good day. A normal day. Just what we all needed. More days like this and the horrors of the last couple of weeks would fade. And life was good too, opening up to a future of welcome possibilities.

Half listening to a local man who had cornered me by the drinks table and was now singing the praises of my radio show, I sipped my wine and watched Nathan sharing a joke with Lowe and some of the men under his command over by the buffet table. He was chewing on a chicken leg and looked more relaxed than I had seen him in a long time. The sound of his laughter carried across the room. My throat tightened. What kind of fool must I have been to let him go?

I checked my watch. Time I was heading home. Though, hopefully London wouldn't be home for much longer. I made my excuses to the exuberant local and said my goodbyes to Karen and Lowe, avoiding more of Karen's questions about my plans, and interrupted Nathan to let him know I was leaving.

He made his excuses and walked me out to the car.

He'd grown serious again. Something was on his mind.

We reached the car and he said, "You know I've never been one to rush things."

"And you don't want to rush us." I slow-punched his arm. "It's okay. I get it. And some things are worth waiting for."

"It's been a long time. And maybe we need to take things a step at a time. Get to know each other again."

"I'm okay with that. And who knows, I may even find you've improved over the years."

"I wouldn't bet on it."

"I'm not going to."

"I know I ...I know I'm not one of the easiest people to get on with. I know I can be a bit - you know - heavy-handed at times."

"No," I said, in my best sarcastic tone. "I would never have guessed."

He bristled at that. "Listen, Prince Charming. You're not so easy-going yourself. You can be a real pain in the arse sometimes."

"I never pretended otherwise."

A heartbeat later, we were smiling at each other.

"Are we always going to be arguing like this?" he said.

"Probably."

His face creased into a grin. "I guess I'd better get used to it then."

"I guess we both had."

I reached up and ran the back of my hand down his face. That strong handsome face. And an overwhelming surge of emotion welled up inside me. A mixture of sadness and joy. Sadness for the lost years. For the self-denial. For being too much of a coward to stand up for what I wanted. And joy for the great good fortune at having, at last, found my way back home.

My eyes watered.

His smile changed to a look of concern. "Hey, why so sad?"

I shrugged. "I can be so stupid at times."

"I already knew that," he said, grinning again.

For once I wasn't going to argue.

He pressed his lips to my forehead. "Just hurry back."

Now I was smiling. "Soon as I can. I'll be counting the days. And this time, no one's going to keep me away. This time, it's for keeps."

Still smiling, I climbed into the Elan, took one last look at the man I loved, the man I had always loved, and drove away.

IF YOU ENJOYED THIS BOOK

I'm hard at work writing the next title in this series which continues to follow the ups and downs of Mikey and Nathan's troubled relationship. If you enjoyed this book, you may wish to add your name to my mailing list to receive notification of publication.

Please see details on my Website
GrantAtherton.co.uk

And I'd love it if you could post a review about the book on Amazon or another website. Getting reviews would give me a lot of pleasure and I look forward to reading what you think. Perhaps you could mention which parts you liked best.

I look forward to hearing from you

Grant Atherton

Printed in Great Britain
by Amazon